HER REASON
TO STAY

BY
ANNA ADAMS

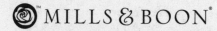

All the characters in this book have no existence outside the imagination of the author, and have no relation whatsoever to anyone bearing the same name or names. They are not even distantly inspired by any individual known or unknown to the author, and all the incidents are pure invention.

First published in Great Britain 2010
Harlequin Mills & Boon Limited,
Eton House, 18-24 Paradise Road, Richmond, Surrey TW9 1SR

© Anna Adams 2008

ISBN: 978 0 263 87958 2

23-0310

Harlequin Mills & Boon policy is to use papers that are natural, renewable and recyclable products and made from wood grown in sustainable forests. The logging and manufacturing processes conform to the legal environmental regulations of the country of origin.

Printed and bound in Spain
by Litografia Rosés S.A., Barcelona

Anna Adams wrote her first romance on the beach in wet sand with a stick. The Atlantic Ocean washed that one away, but these days she uses modern tools to write the kind of stories she loves best – romance that involves everyone in the family, and often the whole community. Anna is in the middle of one of those stories with her own hero of twenty-seven years. From Iceland to Hawaii and points in between they've shared their lives with children and family and friends who've become family. Right now they're living in a small Southern town, whose square has become the model for the one where much of the action happens in Honesty, Virginia. In fact, Anna wrote much of *Her Reason To Stay* in a coffee shop looking out at the courthouse that readers of this series must know so well.

To Colin and his Sarah,
who, happily, is another Sarah for us to love.
Buddy, the instant I first looked into your face,
I became a better woman. Have I ever
thanked you for that?

CHAPTER ONE

"I CAN HARDLY LOOK at you. You have my face. And seeing you reminds me that my parents lied to me."

Those weren't exactly the words she wanted to hear. Daphne Soder had expected surprise, maybe even shock from her long-lost sister. Instead, the stranger who was also her twin seemed one second away from leaping out the closest window.

Ignoring a strong urge to stop her, Daphne kept still, trying not to frighten Raina Abernathy any further.

Raina sat beside her lawyer, barricaded behind a long maple conference table in the office of Delaney, Brock, Sheffield and Gannon. Her body language screamed, "stay away," as she moved closer to the dark-haired man whom she clearly considered her protector.

His name was Patrick Gannon, and his glacial expression pierced Daphne as if he expected her to reach across the table and murder Raina in front of him.

So much for a happy reunion. Daphne had arrived at this meeting filled with the crazy hope that she and her sister could finally become a family, that they'd learn to love each other. But Raina obviously didn't want that, and her rejection hurt.

"I'm sorry. I had no idea you didn't know about the adoption," Daphne said. "Still, that doesn't change why I'm here."

Patrick turned toward her, his mouth a thin line, his glare raising goose bumps that made her hug herself. He stared at her arms, then looked into her eyes, his own filling with suspicion.

"I don't have any ulterior motives," she said. "But I hope you aren't thinking like Mr. Gannon, Raina." She met his gaze full on. It took more than a man with the ability to launch an ice age at a glance to scare her these days. "Or are you assuming the worst because my sister does?"

Neither Patrick nor Raina answered.

"I'd hoped you'd welcome the chance to meet your twin sister," Daphne continued. "I understand you're reluctant because you don't know me, but can't you try?" She studied Raina—a polished, expensive yet timid version of herself.

Raina looked away, but not before Daphne saw her obvious sadness. She reminded herself that she'd had months to get accustomed to the idea that she had a twin sister. And because her family had been anything but stable, the news had been welcome. The same was not true for Raina, who probably was struggling to accept such a radical change to her world. That realization nudged aside Daphne's disappointment, allowing her to feel Raina's pain.

Almost against her will, Daphne slid her hand

across the table toward Raina. Reaching out to strangers was difficult, but she and Raina shared a bond that Daphne longed to build on. Offering physical support was a monumental step she had to take.

Patrick shifted, positioning his body to protect Raina. The rejection and hostility in the move, along with Raina's acquiescence made Daphne snatch back her hand.

He glanced at Raina, and the look they exchanged appeared intimate, as if they carried out a silent conversation. Certainly their closeness exceeded the bounds of a typical lawyer-client relationship. He seemed ready to vanquish dragons—or in this case, a pesky, lowbrow twin who didn't have the sense to stay hidden—at the merest gesture from Raina. Daphne knew a moment of envy. A woman who had Patrick Gannon in her corner would never need a pit bull or an electric fence to keep her safe. Did Raina appreciate having someone so willing to support her? Did she know the value of not having to fight battles alone?

Daphne tucked both hands under the table and twisted her fingers until they hurt. She didn't need a man like Patrick in her life. She knew how to take care of herself. In fact, she preferred it that way.

"I can't give you money," Raina spoke suddenly, startling Daphne. "It's all tied up. In a trust. I just get an allowance."

"You think I'm letting you treat me like this because I want your cash?"

Patrick opened the folder in front of him. "It's a

logical conclusion. Raina has inherited the Abernathy pharmaceutical fortune. And from what I've been able to discover, you don't have many assets of your own."

Her beleaguered finances were no secret. But if that was the biggest obstacle Patrick could throw in her path, then clearly he hadn't been that thorough in his background check. If he knew her true history, he never would have allowed her within the same state as Raina. Still, those deeds were in her past and bore little relevance to this situation, even though she doubted Patrick and Raina would hold the same view.

"You have nothing compared to the Abernathy fortune," Raina said.

Her coldness and the way she stressed her adopted family name destroyed Daphne's dreams of an amicable reunion and a new family. So she reacted the way she usually did in the face of rejection—she went on the offensive.

"You have everything," Daphne said. "Wealth, poise and standing in this little town. I'll bet your parents loved you and made sure you had nothing but the best." In essence, all the things that were in such short supply in Daphne's life. "Yet despite those advantages, I can't detect a shred of kindness in you. It's a disappointment to think we share the same blood."

"You counted on kindness? You expected to be welcomed with open arms because we resemble each other? Blood doesn't make us family."

Daphne brushed her bangs out of her eyes. "This is not how I saw meeting you."

"Tell us what you want," Patrick said, halting the deteriorating conversation.

Daphne resisted looking to Raina for help. If their roles had been reversed, Daphne would have told him to stay out of the situation and let her talk to her sister. But after her quick insults, Raina was content to leave the hard work to her lawyer. One more piece of evidence that their physical similarities did not extend to their personalities.

Honesty, Virginia, had sounded like a sanctuary to Daphne from the moment she'd read about it and Raina. A chance to create the kind of family most people took for granted. Finding out that she was a twin had underscored her loneliness and isolation.

Raina hadn't been alone. She'd had a mother and a father who'd loved her. She'd been a princess in this town. She'd belonged to people and to a place. She'd never needed that mystical twin connection the way Daphne had. Raina hadn't needed fantasies of real parents swooping in to rescue her from a crazy foster mother who beat her with wooden spoons. Or from a foster mother's boyfriend who seemed a little too interested in the young female charges. The disparity in their childhoods and their biological connection motivated Daphne. She wanted, no, *needed,* Raina to acknowledge her.

"I've searched for our parents for years." Ten years to be precise. Since she'd turned eighteen. "I finally learned our mother died in a car accident soon after we were born. Our father gave us up for adoption. I haven't traced him, but I found out about you in a newspaper clipping. The article talked about our mother's accident and mentioned her surviving twin daughters."

"*My* mother died three months ago," Raina snapped. "It's too late to start wondering about this other—woman."

"You can't help feeling—" Daphne said.

"Don't pity me." Raina's voice went shrill.

Daphne stared at her, surprised to feel the tightness of tears. Regardless of her treatment of Daphne, Raina was mourning. "I don't," she said.

"Who needs your pity? My parents loved me. They didn't tell me about this other life I barely had because they knew what you don't understand. That past has no relevance. It's not me."

Maybe the Abernathys hadn't wanted anything to mar the illusion of their perfect life. Or maybe they had been afraid Raina couldn't handle the truth, which her oh-so-helpful sister had brought home with a vengeance.

Either way, it appeared Raina wasn't content to hide behind Patrick for the entire meeting. Not about to let the two of them tag-team her, Daphne turned to him.

"Why are you here?"

Her aggressive tone made Raina sit back in obvious surprise, while Patrick gave a startled half smile that increased the laugh lines around his mouth and eyes. She couldn't help thinking that if he knew how much the expression softened him, he'd never use it. She liked how that simple curving of his lips hinted at warmth hidden beneath his cold exterior.

Without warning or any reason, he woke a new emotion in Daphne. A longing that baffled her. She hadn't come here to get all fascinated by a man whose job it was to thwart her.

"Patrick's with me in case I need him to explain the facts of my life to you," Raina said. "I have nothing to share with you."

"Nothing? No sister's love? No interest in finding out if we could be a family?"

Daphne wished she hadn't spoken. Raina's silence was more than enough answer. Daphne looked out the rain-streaked windows at budding treetops and the bell tower of the courthouse that composed the town's square. She'd never forget this moment. Her quest to build a future with her sister ended now.

Even in the face of her pain, she refused to let these two, with their suspicions and remote expressions, know she hurt. She faced them, trying to appear as if she didn't care.

Raina couldn't look at her. Her eyes flickered toward Patrick, no doubt seeking his support. Money, even tied up in a trust, mattered to Raina. Money. If she'd worried about anything else, Daphne would have been willing to fight. But she would never tolerate being accused of acting out of greed.

She banged her hands on the table and pushed back her chair. On her feet, she was aware of her faded jeans and knit shirt. By comparison, Raina's white suit must have cost more than the rent Daphne had paid last year.

"I'm leaving, but I want you to remember I only asked for family. Goodbye, Raina."

Patrick stood—to make sure she didn't pick her sister's pocket on the way out? "Wait," he said. "Why don't you—"

"No." She wanted out of this room with its smells of polish and coffee and paper. She needed fresh air that wasn't weighed down with judgment and skepticism.

Her sneakers made no sound on the plush mushroom-colored carpet. She opened the door and slipped through. The receptionist sprang from her chair, mistaking Daphne for someone who mattered.

She held her head high, startled that no one recognized her as a woman limping on the last of her courage. At the elevator, she punched the down button. Four times. Fast.

The conference-room door opened. No way would she check to see who'd exited the den of intimidation.

She made for the door marked Stairs. She pounded down, half sliding on the metal balustrade, praying she'd come out in an alley rather than the foyer.

The gods must have been playing with her. At the bottom she stumbled straight into the marble atrium of Blah-Blah-Blah-and-Gannon.

The latter burst out of the elevator so abruptly the doors rattled on their runners. Swearing beneath her breath, Daphne walked quickly. She wouldn't run, but she wanted out of this building before Patrick caught her.

He beat her to the revolving door, stepping in front of her. He held out his hands. "I don't think you understand."

"I didn't. I do now."

"I'm all Raina has left, but that doesn't mean I don't give a damn about anyone else. And Raina doesn't want to hurt you."

Daphne stared at him. "You see a different Raina than I did."

Patrick smiled. A hint of sensuality curved his lips, but she didn't want to respond to it.

"Don't leave like this," he said.

"I don't blame her. We don't know each other, and I just blew up all her beliefs about her happy family."

"She doesn't want you to go."

"Since when?"

"I guess since she realized you really were walking away."

"So she changed her mind a split second ago." Not good enough. Daphne deserved better than a half-hearted plea delivered by someone else. "You know, that sentiment might be more convincing if she'd had the guts to deliver it herself."

Patrick took her arm. She pulled away with a you-die look that had always stood her in good stead.

"We were cold to you," he said.

"You have a talent for cold."

"Think of the coincidence. Raina's mother died and the estate went to her. It's been well publicized."

"You'd be surprised how few Honesty newspapers sally beyond the town limits. That, combined with the fact I don't read the financial pages, means I didn't know Raina was rich."

He glanced toward the passersby who eyed them curiously. "Out of nowhere—" he lowered his voice "—you arrive, claiming Raina's family wasn't really hers, but that you are."

"It sounds improbable right now, but until I saw the two of you sitting behind that table as if you were under siege, I assumed she'd be as happy as I was to find a sister."

For a moment, he said nothing. Upstairs, he'd been as impassive as Raina. But now he looked uncomfortable.

"Raina and I made assumptions, too," he said. "Come back up, and we'll all start over."

"Forget it. I made a mistake."

"I'm trying to explain what we thought. Raina's mother asked me to protect her. I have to do that."

"She's a grown woman."

"And totally untouched. Honesty is a safe place where few things have challeneged her. She's used to her life being a certain way and you've changed that. But she is a good person. Get to know her, and see what I mean." He touched her again, squeezing her wrist as if to emphasize his sincerity. She looked down, causing him to release her.

"You all but accused me of planning to rob Raina the second she turns her back on an open check-book." His intensity had the strange effect of a rope around her throat. She was strong enough to ignore a passing attraction to some guy. She wouldn't let him distract her. "You think I'm after my sister's money. I don't need it. I can find a job. I've found a way to start over too many times to tell you." Good God. It was like in the old days, when she'd drink too much and buttonhole strangers to confess her worst sins. "I never found family before."

She didn't realize her voice had broken until he lowered his head. Above him, the atrium soared to a glass dome. His dark lashes glinted in the diffused light. No doubt part of Mother Nature's foul plan to make him look sensitive.

"I have to go," she said.

"I know I'm making this worse, but I just want to ask for another chance. For Raina," he said. "Accept our apologies for thinking you might be here for whatever handout she could give you."

"I don't see how you stay in business. The other attorneys must rake you over in court if you're this articulate."

"I hardly ever make a fool of myself like this." He stepped out of her way. She could have left.

"Why should I stay? Raina didn't care enough to come downstairs to insult me, herself. None of what you or I say matters because this is between me and her."

She got as far as the revolving door.

"Raina's still mourning her mother. Her father died when she was in college. She has no one else."

Daphne was already reaching for the door, but she thought of Raina, braced behind the big table, her arms wrapped around her waist. His shot hit Daphne right where she was weakest.

"No one," he said again.

Maybe he wasn't that bad in court. "You know things about me. Have you investigated me?"

"No," he said. He was a good liar, but she'd been a jury consultant. She'd made her living sitting in on voir dire to assess which jurors would vote her client's way in a court case. She understood psychology and body language, and she was hard to fool. She eyed him steadily until he continued. "I looked. Aside from the financials, I found stuff on your track-and-field results."

She almost told him he hadn't dug deep enough, but why send him straight to the truth about her past? He and Raina would think even less of her.

"She's alone. You could help her. She might help you, too."

"Alone's a bad place to be."

A man in a business suit burst through the door from outside, shaking rain off his umbrella. Patrick pulled her away from the door.

"People have already tried to take advantage of Raina."

"I don't doubt that." It was the way of the world. "But I didn't, and I wouldn't have. I shouldn't have come here. This place... It makes me think of families and old-fashioned closeness. I'm used to bad guys who wear their evil on their sleeves." She couldn't articulate her experience of the town thus far. Of course, her exposure had been limited, so maybe she should see more before passing judgment. "My sister is content in a world I'm not sure I could live in even if I wanted to. I'm used to larger, more anonymous cities."

"How do you know until you try?"

"It might be pointless, Patrick."

She hadn't meant to say his name. It was too personal. It invited proximity. As if acting on that invitation, he stepped closer. Her awareness of her surroundings narrowed until she saw—felt—only Patrick.

Each breath pressed his chest against her shoulder. The situation grew personal in the extreme.

"You don't know this place. Raina's been lost since her mother died. You could help her life make sense again. I can't do any more for her."

He wasn't acting the part of a knight in a business suit. He truly cared about Raina. His love for her dragged Daphne back to earth with a thump.

She twisted away. "I don't understand what goes on between you two, but *you* make me feel claustrophobic."

"I don't understand."

Maybe he'd never longed for that one person who made him feel he had a place, a love stronger than anything else he'd ever known—a love to fill the gaps created by years without affection or concern. But Daphne had. And she began to suspect that Patrick loved Raina that much.

Daphne hadn't resented Raina's luckier ticket in the adoption lottery, and she'd been glad her sister had never been forced to fend off unwanted male attention. Right now Daphne envied the connection between Raina and this man.

"I'm sorry." Daphne held out her hand. "You're my sister's answer. She doesn't want love from me. You matter to her. Goodbye, Mr. Gannon."

He stared at her for a moment, the look in his eyes confused as his hand clasped hers. Her palm disappeared in his. Her fingers felt crushed and her arm grew heavy from her wrist to her shoulder. Heavy with awareness.

"I didn't expect you to be like this," Patrick said. "You're strong enough to walk away."

She retreated, fighting her attraction. A woman who'd grown up with inappropriate men, Daphne recognized the danger of being vulnerable to a man like Patrick—one who got through her defenses, one who was committed elsewhere. Affairs always started this way. Sexual longing. Looking too deeply into his eyes. Him holding her hand too long, drawing out perfectly natural physical contact, making it something more. That path, however tempting, led to heartache. It led away from the real, safe love she deserved.

She should run, if only because of Patrick and the threat of a relationship that had nothing to do with her reasons for coming to Honesty.

But there was Raina. Suppose he was right. Suppose she really wanted to know Daphne, but she didn't know how to say so.

Wasn't it worth another day or two in this little town to have the chance to know her sister?

"I'll stay."

Instead of sagging with relief, he seemed to grow larger. His shoulders went back as he took a deep breath.

"But she has to call me. She has to make the next move." Daphne had a right to make demands after the way they'd treated her. "And next time we meet on neutral ground."

Before he could counter or touch her again in a way that would persuade her to linger, she left. She walked to where she'd parked, ignoring the rain. She tried to look purposeful, as if she weren't trembling from scalp to toe with unexpected, totally illogical need of a man who loved her sister.

CHAPTER TWO

"DID YOU CATCH HER?"

"I caught her." Patrick pressed his tingling palm to the side of his jacket.

What was his problem? Daphne was his client's sister. Besides, he wasn't interested in a relationship right now. There'd been plenty of women who'd offered to comfort the poor, divorced single dad whose ex-wife had loved pills better than their family.

He'd turned down those women because his son needed him and he couldn't afford to complicate his life any further. But something about Daphne had almost made him forget.

With ridiculous weakness, he'd basked in her scent, eased closer so that the dark tendrils of her hair had curled against his shoulder, while he'd kept her talking, not only to persuade her to give Raina a second chance, but to prolong the pleasure of drowning in the whiskey-honey tones of her voice.

He'd been too long on his own with his son, Will.

"She's staying, but you have to call her, Raina. I'm done."

"I will." Raina pushed herself out of her chair.

Happiness softened the pinched lines of her face as she hurried to the window.

Patrick had worried about her since the moment her mother had pulled him closer to her hospital bed and begged him to look after her daughter. It was good to see those lines ease.

Nevertheless, he had to make sure she understood he wasn't part of her relationship with Daphne, whatever it turned out to be.

"You're too late," he said as Raina's forehead bumped the window. "She was speed walking last time I saw her." He'd probably lit the fire—hanging on to her as if she were a rope at the edge of quicksand.

"I didn't know what to say." Raina pressed fingertips to her head. "She looks like me, but she…she seems so different."

Raina was right. Daphne *was* different. She was strong, independent and, most telling, she wasn't afraid to let her feelings be known.

At twenty-eight, Raina remained, improbably, the princess under glass in one of Will's Disney movies.

"You know where she's staying?"

"She sent me the address." Raina dug in her purse. "Even after your secretary told her to get in touch with you if she wanted to meet today."

"She doesn't take orders well."

"You admire her, Patrick?"

Admire her? He shrugged. "She's got courage. She's had a harder life than you."

He needn't have been so blunt. Daphne had rattled him, resurrected feelings he'd thought had gone forever. He'd deliberately kept his emotions on ice after what had happened to his son last year. Staying detached from everyone except Raina and Will had become his special skill.

"How do you go to someone you've never met and tell her you're her twin? And how do you anticipate being welcomed?" Raina found what she was looking for, a crumpled envelope. "I admire her courage, but I don't have it in me to love a sister who's a stranger."

"I'll repeat what I said to her. Give her a chance."

"You asked *her* to give *me* a chance?" Raina looked affronted at the idea that she had done something that required being given a second chance.

Which was Patrick's last straw. He should have walked when Raina had first called him about her twin-out-of-nowhere. Untouched by life except in her own extraordinary home, she might be out of her depth with a woman like Daphne.

Patrick began to gather the papers around his folder, still open on the table. "Raina, I've paved the way for you. The rest is up to you."

Raina waved off his impatience. "I know. I get upset about the wrong things, and I always look to you to help me make a decision, but my mother's not here, and I can't ask her why she didn't tell me I was adopted. She should have warned me. She had to know Daphne or my birth parents might show up."

"No one came in all these years. Hannah probably thought her secret was safe."

"Okay, okay." Raina gripped the envelope so hard

it crinkled in the silent room. "Why do you suppose they didn't adopt Daphne, too?"

"I don't know. You were infants. Maybe your parents didn't know about Daphne."

"Does that seem likely?"

"I'd think the agency would have wanted sisters to go together."

"Just when I need my memories most, I feel as if I didn't know my parents, either." Raina straightened the envelope and pulled out the letter. "I'll call Daphne's hotel." She scanned the writing. "Good Lord, it's one of those cheap ones out on Helier Drive."

Patrick had noticed the frayed cuffs of Daphne's long-sleeved T-shirt and the worn spots on her jeans. Those shiny white patches, forming the seat of her pants, would stay on his mind a while, but he couldn't attribute them to her sense of style.

"That hotel is probably all she can afford." He wasn't any happier than Raina at the thought of Daphne in an area where most of Honesty's criminal activities occurred.

"I wonder if she'd meet me for coffee?"

"Ask her." He glanced at his watch. "I have some meetings."

"Why are you so eager to rush off? We didn't intend to hurt her feelings."

"It got out of hand fast. We should have been more tactful." Accusing Daphne right at the start of wanting money had been unfair. "She wants to get to know you. You're interested in finding out about her. If you talk, things will work out."

Raina took out her cell phone. "Mind if I use this room a second longer?"

"Fine. Will's waiting for me." His mother looked after Will, and Patrick was already late to pick up his son. He shoved the last of the loose pages inside the folder he'd made on Daphne. Sports clippings from the Internet, bank statements, her initial letter to Raina, hope written between every line. "Take your time and try to keep the games to a minimum, Raina."

"Games?"

"You know what I mean. This morning was a game. You tried to make Daphne angry enough to admit she'd come to take advantage of you. But maybe she didn't."

She stopped in the middle of punching in Daphne's number on her phone. "What happened downstairs?"

"Nothing happened," he said. Nothing would. Will was his priority.

But from the second he'd read hurt in Daphne's eyes, from the moment he'd held her hand too long, he'd wanted her, pure and—not in any way—simple.

How, out of the blue, could he desire a stranger when he'd sworn off any attachment except to Will until they had their life under control again?

"Patrick?" Raina dropped the phone to her side. "You look funny. Are you okay?" She put her hand on the table, leaning toward him. "Is Will all right?"

He turned the legal pad and folder as if aligning their edges were a priority. Raina knew he still felt guilty that his son had almost died because he'd been blind to his ex-wife's addiction. If he'd known how much Lisa had craved the drugs that had become her crutch, he'd never have left Will alone with her. And his son would have been safely at home that snowy day, rather than nearly dying of hypothermia in the backseat of the car while his mother lay unconscious in a dressing room less than a block from Patrick's office.

"Will's fine." Raina had witnessed the rapid divorce that left him with custody of his son. She might be focused on her own grief, but she could step outside it long enough to care about his family. That was why he went out of his way for her.

"Daphne didn't come for money." He hoped he wasn't mistaking his own lust for good judgment. "I believe her."

"Why?"

"She wouldn't have walked out of here if she'd planned to work you for a paycheck."

"Something changed. You were on my side, but suddenly Daphne's strong and kind, and I'm not supposed to play games."

"We're talking trust. You both want to know each other, and that's going to take trust." He reached for the door then turned to look at her. She was right in a way. Those few minutes with Daphne had changed his feelings. It didn't make sense and it wasn't con-venient. "I didn't mean to hurt you, Raina."

She'd always been the younger sister he'd never had, but the image of her twin, using her body to push through the revolving door, made him hitch his shoul-ders beneath a shirt that suddenly tormented his skin.

He'd looked at Raina almost every day of her life. He'd talked to her and laughed with her and protected her, but Daphne was different. Her sad eyes had made him wonder about the secrets hiding behind them. He had felt the taut weight of her breasts, a breath away from his chest, as if he'd held her already.

After living alone with his son for long, empty, safe months, he'd longed to wrap his arms around Daphne's slender waist and simply take pleasure in her warmth and curves.

Wouldn't he be safe with a woman who wanted family as badly as she did? Did he dare even entertain the possibility? After such deep acquaintance with fear and anger, hope seemed to sting.

"I've got to get to Will," he said.

LATER THAT DAY, Daphne inhaled the coffee aroma, trying not to be noticed by the woman and little girl in line in front of her, not wanting them to mistake her for Raina. She checked her watch. She'd arrived at Cosmic Grounds about fifteen minutes early for her appointment with her sister, but it gave her time to appreciate the dark wood wainscoting beneath rich red walls without gawking like the stranger she was.

She eyed buttery-smelling scones on plates beside jars of biscotti and chocolate-chip cookies wrapped in crinkly sleeves. The little girl plucked a praline out of a pyramid of the fat caramel-colored candies.

"Can I have one, Mommy?"

Her mother glanced down, barely comprehending. "I guess." Then she looked startled when the girl behind the counter asked for more money.

Daphne risked a scan of the other customers, a man buried behind a newspaper, a young girl running her index finger over a tome the size of the Domesday Book. The girl sipped her coffee. Her short cap of brown hair fell away from her face, and she smiled with tired gray eyes.

Daphne had worked her way through a criminology degree. She recognized the signs of unremitting study. The girl went back to her work, and Daphne sighed, hoping despite a healthy dose of wariness that this might become her favorite coffee shop.

Cosmic Grounds didn't compare in size or even selection to the chain coffee shop down the block. Interesting that Raina had chosen it for their meeting. She seemed conventional all the way. Maybe she was hoping that the two of them wouldn't be seen by too many of her neighbors.

The mother and daughter hurried from the shop, balancing a coffee cup, a small container of hot cocoa and the girl's candy.

Daphne didn't realize she'd been watching them until she turned back to find the spiky-haired blonde behind the counter staring at her. Daphne glanced over her shoulder again before she realized the college-aged young woman must have thought she was Raina.

"Hey."

"Hey," the girl said, but then slapped her hand

over her mouth as if she'd dared too much. Was Raina a snob?

Daphne slid her hands inside her jean pockets. "I'm not my sister" almost slipped out of her mouth. But even as the idea of Raina intimidating coffee-shop employees troubled her, she didn't want to criticize her sister.

Forget it. The good citizens of Honesty would soon find there were two of them, and this girl could expect the shock any moment.

The girl lifted her khaki Cosmic Grounds baseball cap and settled it again on her spiky hairdo. "Can I help you?"

"May I have a café au lait and a cherry scone?"

"Sure." Smacking a big wad of gum, she tapped out the charges and gave Daphne the bill, still studying her. "I'll bring it to your table."

Daphne paid then found a spot for two in a dark corner. Until she knew how Raina felt, it might be best to keep their meeting private.

Trying to be invisible reminded Daphne of how she'd spent her adolescence, hunched over, pre-tending she wasn't a developing young woman, that she didn't exist, hoping no one else would try to touch her.

She was spending her twenties learning to live confidently in her own skin.

A small hand with a Celtic ring tattooed in henna on its index finger slid a mug and scone onto the table.

"I like that." Daphne pointed to the girl's finger.

"*You* like it?"

Daphne almost laughed. Raina must not seem like a tattoo kind of girl. The door opened, making the bell above it peal. The girl turned to greet her new customer. Only to wheel back and eye Daphne.

"I thought you were her."

"You're probably wondering why now." Seeing them both, no one would have trouble telling the sophisticated, well-groomed Raina from Daphne.

"Hunh." The girl whistled around her gum and went back to the counter.

Even Daphne felt confused when she looked at her twin. Daphne's hair tended to clench like a fist in the rain, so she'd wound it into a knot before she'd climbed out of her car. Raina's hair dared not curl. If they ever became intimate enough, Daphne would ask how her sister achieved such flawless control.

Raina placed her order then came to the table. She tucked her change into a wallet that matched her multibuckled, oversize white purse. "Sorry I kept you waiting. I couldn't find my umbrella. I never used to be so scattered." Not one wrinkle, not a speck of dirt touched her white suit.

Daphne marveled. Nature versus nurture. They were bound to learn which was more powerful if they got to know each other.

"You're staring," Raina said.

Daphne shut her mouth. "Not to be rude. Why'd you ask me to meet you here?"

"You get to the point."

"I thought the same thing about you in Patrick's office." She must have said his name with some special emphasis because Raina lifted both eyebrows, leaning forward. Daphne touched her own brows.

"Patrick talked you into giving me a second chance," Raina said. "How did he do that?"

Daphne picked a packet of sweetener out of a small ceramic holder. "He said you'd want to know me."

Raina stared at the sweetener package for a second. "I'm sorry about accusing you, but I have money, and you…"

"Don't. But I do have a temper." And pride. "I have manners and feelings, despite my low-class background."

"Right. Sorry." She took the sweetener out of Daphne's fingers, and Daphne met her sister's gaze.

Again, Raina said nothing for several moments. Finally, she held her hand out. "I behaved like an idiot, but please take some time before you decide about me."

Daphne took her hand. They shook as the girl from the counter approached with a tray.

Raina took it, her expression relaxing into a smile. "Thanks, Kyla." She set her mug—tea—and a dish of sugar cubes on the table.

"Sure." Kyla took the tray back, still staring from one to the other of them. "Call me if you need anything else."

Raina grinned at Kyla's retreating back. "She's shocked. So am I, every time I look at you."

"But you seem to be taking it in stride now." Daphne sipped her coffee. "I thought you were frightened this afternoon. Now, you seem confident, like a woman with a plan."

"My parents never told me I was adopted. Imagine opening a door and seeing someone with your face who tells you the last thing you want to hear."

"What did you think? That I'd had plastic surgery or something to make myself look like you so you'd give me money?"

"I'm not suggesting we aren't twins, but I've learned to be suspicious of everyone. I've already had guys ask me to marry them. Not because I'm so lovable." She shrugged, and Daphne admired her ability to laugh at herself. "Which you may have noticed. But they each desired a piece of my net worth. My life is ludicrous, and you show up when I'm feeling most cynical."

"When is a bad time to find family? All I wanted was to know my sister."

That word felt strange to Daphne, not warm anymore. Raina ignored it.

"I do a lot of things well." She dropped a couple of sugar cubes into her cup, and then she dipped her tea bag. "My mother taught me to pretend people aren't staring at me and my companion in a coffee shop. She trained me to wear the right clothes for spring, although she probably would have checked the weather forecast before she put on white. She taught me how to appear cool under fire." She tilted her head at a wry angle. "Only, I seem to have a problem with that one, too."

"You're not under fire. I want to know if we can be sisters." A knot in her throat stopped her. She didn't want Raina to realize how much it mattered.

But Raina noticed. "That's what I mean. I don't know how I'm supposed to respond. My parents lied to me. You're looking for someone who could be your family. I've just lost the last of mine, and here you are, suggesting we could belong together."

Belong together. Even Daphne hadn't gone that far. Her heartbeat picked up a little pace. Speaking became difficult. This was why she'd come to Honesty.

Raina stirred her tea without touching the sides of the mug and set the spoon delicately on a paper napkin.

Suddenly, there was something Daphne had to know. "Did Patrick make you call me? He came after me because *he* was worried. This meeting was his idea."

Raina looked straight at her for the first time. "You call him Patrick as if you know each other."

Had he noticed she was attracted to him? "Should I have said Mr. Gannon?" What had Patrick said after he'd gone back upstairs? Had they laughed at her?

"That's not what I meant, but you two spent a few minutes alone in an elevator, and suddenly you're both different."

Worse than laughing. "I took the stairs."

Raina looked confused, but then she laughed, picking up her spoon again. She gave her tea another stir. "I overreacted. To you and to everything about our situation."

"Being sisters? That situation?" Or was Raina staking her claim to Patrick? Suddenly, Daphne couldn't breathe. She felt around for her own purse.

"What are you doing?"

"Getting out of here, once and for all. You don't care that we're sisters. You called only because you do what Patrick says."

"No, no, no." Raina said it as she would chide a young child, and she reached for Daphne's wrist. She looked down. "My God, you're thin. Don't you ever get a square meal?"

Daphne wanted to run, but if she did, she'd never see Raina again. It was too much to risk.

"Will you let me say I'm sorry?" Raina let Daphne go, but her steady gaze suggested she might grab at Daphne again if she made a move toward the door.

Maybe they were both overreacting.

"Sorry," Daphne said. "Maybe I seem confident, but trust isn't my strong suit." She wrapped her hand around her throat. Moments like this made her thirsty for more than just coffee.

"That's something we share."

Daphne flattened her hands on the table. "We share?" She hardly knew she'd said it out loud until Raina's mouth began to move.

"Four guys, Daphne. Four requests to help themselves to the Abernathy portfolio, all during the past three months. And I've known these men since I was a child." She sipped her tea. Her mouth was so tight, Daphne half expected the liquid to trickle down her chin. "One was a friend of my father's. His age."

Daphne slid her hands up her arms, over goose bumps. "I feel the ick factor, but you didn't understand me." Being blunt felt awkward. "I want to share—things—our past, the lives we want, the truth—with you. I want a real relationship, not a nodding acquaintance."

She stuttered to a halt, but Raina's smile switched on. "You have weaknesses, too."

"That makes you happy?" That she was vulnerable? That one person left in the world could hurt her?

"No, not happy. But I can identify with you. I may look capable, but something happened to me after my mother's—death." Raina's sadness made Daphne long to comfort her, but Raina had a formidable touch-me-not air. "As you saw in Patrick's office, sometimes I'm barely able to function. I'm wondering where you get your guts, why you have them but I don't."

Daphne smiled. "That's a funny word from you."

"Courage, if you prefer."

"I wonder whether we're both brave enough to try being sisters." Daphne eyed Raina over the rim of her coffee cup.

Raina drank her tea, honest-to-God splaying her little finger, then she set the cup in its saucer.

"Let's get your things." She pulled her suitcase-purse close to her chest.

"My things?" Raina had gone from shrinking in Patrick's office to bossing the sister she hadn't fully accepted yet. Daphne grabbed her coffee, telling herself it was too soon to move in together. "I can't stay with you."

Raina arched her perfect eyebrows. "You don't have a job. Where can you afford to—"

"I have a room in a hotel. I sent you the address."

"That place isn't safe for a rat."

Daphne ran a finger over her eyebrows, which could have benefited from the waxing Raina had obviously recently endured. "Don't let anyone say you're not a plain speaker."

"I'm just suggesting you'd feel more comfortable, and we'd have more time together if you came home with me."

"Just a few hours ago you accused me of trying to rob you. It's pretty hard to forget what you said."

"About?"

"Not having money for me, Raina. Now *you* want to adopt me. But you and your buddy Patrick might talk it over in a few days and decide I'd tricked you into giving me a room in your ritzy house."

"Come on. I didn't react well. Would you have done any better?"

Daphne stared at her. "I honestly don't know. I'm very aware that I'm the bad bargain in this deal."

"Bad bargain? What are you talking about?"

"Are you serious? Look at me. My clothes are rags compared to yours. My tastes are plebeian. I have nothing to give you."

"I haven't asked for anything."

"Except to be left alone."

"That's over. Let's think of how you can find a way to live here. You need a job, a home."

She stopped, her gaze pointed.

"Raina, forget it. You own a palace and I'm peasant material."

"And proud of it." Raina clearly refused to comprehend. "Can you type? I'll bet Patrick could find work for you."

Daphne might have been annoyed if the seductive memory of Patrick's hand sliding over her palm hadn't made her push her fingers under her thighs. Getting close to Patrick would be courting danger. She'd learned a long time ago to ignore instant attraction. Her defenses must be down. "His charity won't do, either. I'll find something."

Raina opened her mouth, but words didn't come.

"You've also changed a lot since this afternoon," Daphne said.

"I'm not stunned anymore." Raina stirred another cube of sugar into her tea. "Now that we agree, come with me and we'll get serious about what to do next."

"We agree?" Raina's enthusiasm put her off. Why had her sister changed her mind so quickly?

Raina ignored her reticence. She flicked the label on her tea bag. "This stuff's horrible. I'll take you to a place that'll serve us something with some taste."

"I can't afford to waste food." Daphne hated the slightly smug, pompous note in her own voice. "Sorry. I mean I can't afford a meal in the kind of restaurant you're talking about."

"Oh." Raina became deeply interested in Daphne's scone. The door opened again, and watery sunlight revealed a pinkish blush on her cheek. "Maybe I'll get one of those." She leaned back, nodding her head to the beat of the jazz tune being played. Her eyes followed the swirls of burgundy and passion-purple paint, cut by dark beams. The lines around her mouth relaxed—almost. "I've never been here, but it's not so bad."

"So how do you know Kyla?"

"We go to the same church." She waved at the young woman behind the counter. Kyla stared as if Raina's chic dark brown coiffure had tilted of its own volition upon her head.

"You have to go up there to get one," Daphne said.

"Really?" Raina sat up, feeling for her purse, but seemingly surprised to find it still in her lap. "Usually they come to me."

Daphne smiled into her cooling coffee as her sister sashayed to the counter.

So far, nurture was winning hands down.

CHAPTER THREE

THAT NIGHT, as the temperature in Daphne's rented room dipped below bone-chilling, she negotiated with the thermostat for more heat. The unit rumbled like a jet on takeoff, and Daphne gagged from the stench of burning dust. She was running for the door to let in fresh air when someone knocked.

The second she touched the chain, it fell out of its slot. She undid the dead bolt and opened the door.

Patrick Gannon stood outside, leaning back for a good look at the overloaded gutters. "You can't stay here," he said.

He hadn't even glanced at her, but she studied his long, lean body, different in jeans and a black sweater. Different, but no less devastating.

"Did you hear me?" he asked.

"It was a hell of a greeting."

He seemed to see her for the first time. Heat invaded his eyes. He could hypnotize an unwary woman with a single glance. But she couldn't force herself to look away.

"One more wet leaf and the roof will cave in." He might have been talking ham sandwiches and coffee. His words didn't affect her half as much as his husky tones.

"I'm not afraid." She shuddered. "Spring's here, so I'm safe until fall." Safe? Not unless she could get rid of him. She had to get a grip. "They're giving me a monthly rate, and I can't afford anything more plush."

He walked in as if she'd invited him. She stepped out of his way.

"The room smells of mold." He crossed to the heat, tapped the vents and then wiped his hands on his legs. "How do you feel about carbon monoxide?"

"Don't say stuff like that. I scare easy." She closed her mouth with a snap. "Honestly, I've stayed in far worse. None of the guests knifed each other in the parking lot last night, and I got a free show." She pointed to the Crowded Beer Case, a drinking establishment whose red neon lights flashed through the gaps in her drapes.

"Maybe you should put in a bid to buy the place." Patrick filled the room with broad, unlawyerly shoulders. His sweater, probably cashmere, hugged his chest and tempted Daphne to run her hands over the muscles so finely delineated.

"All right. It smells bad, and it's not exactly brand new. Why are you here?"

At last he met her eyes. "Raina wants you to stay with her."

"I thought she and I talked this out."

"She knows this place, and she's worried you might not be safe."

"So she sent her mouthpiece again?"

"She always assumes people listen to me because she does."

"And you did manage to stop me from leaving this morning." She said it just to see how he'd react. Was the same half-unwelcome attraction bothering him?

He ignored her comment. "If Raina had any idea what this place was really like, she'd lobby city hall to tear it down."

"I'm fine here."

He shrugged, "give me a break" written all over his face. Daphne shook her head, feeling her skin flush.

"I appreciate that you're both concerned, but I wish she'd stop sending you after me." In the silence, she waited for him to leave. He stood still. "I'm fine," she repeated. "You can tell Raina."

Again, he ignored her jab. "I'd call the biohazard team if the town had one," he said, still eyeing her. He gave a wry smile.

Against her will, she smiled, too. "You're a funny guy." She moved away from him, trying to escape the seduction of his nearness. "But I'm not living off Raina."

"Come work for me. I'll pay you enough to get you out of here."

"Is that another one of Raina's ideas?" She wanted to know about him—why he was so willing to drop everything for Raina. Did he have romantic feelings for her? Was that why he was working so hard to make friends with her? Even giving her a way of supporting herself so she could stay in Honesty.

Daphne reminded herself she was trying to live

her life a new way, without bitterness or resentment. "I'll find a job," she said. "You and Raina don't have to worry about me."

"Why not give my firm a chance?" He caught her arm, as he had that afternoon. She stilled, aware of the heat and heaviness of his hand. "We always need word processing," he continued.

He must not know about her criminology degree or those golden days when her skills had been in demand.

With her free hand, she rubbed her mouth, suddenly thirsty as she remembered the despair of the postacquittal years. She'd never totally managed to drown her sorrow in one bottle after another, but her efforts had nearly destroyed her life.

"What?" A frown etched two small lines into Patrick's forehead. "I don't doubt you're capable." His gaze dropped down her body as if he were brushing fingertips over her skin. Daphne wanted to step behind a barrier, because her breathing and her breasts and her heartbeat had all reacted to his glance.

"What am I doing here?" he asked, his own voice tight.

"That's a good question."

He let her go and stared at his hands as if he'd betrayed himself. "This is your sister's problem. She should have come herself."

"You've done what Raina asked." Seeing his obvious distress, she took pity on him. "Besides, I don't know anything about computers. I've never owned one, so I couldn't do your word processing."

In the way of amateurs everywhere, she'd gone

one lie too many. His skeptical grimace made her laugh with some relief.

"Did I go too far?" she asked.

"Who hasn't used a computer these days?" He touched her hair. The mere heat of his body drew her. She wanted to move closer, so she glued her feet to the floor.

"What did you do before?" he asked.

"Nothing," she said as the past unrolled like film in front of her eyes, the blood, the pain and the disappointment that hurt more than a physical slap. She stepped back, afraid that her memories might somehow leap into Patrick's head. "I searched for Raina. Shouldn't you go now?"

"I want to know," he said, unmoving, but obviously not unmoved. The sympathy in his eyes was more than she could bear.

Something had happened between Patrick Gannon and her. Feelings that ran too deep considering their short duration. "Should we trade?" she asked. "I'll tell you personal things about myself if you do the same."

He backed away, reaching the door with no haste, but sending a message of rejection in his frozen glance. The room fell away behind her.

"Your way may be right," he said. "I had no right to pry. We don't know each other, but I forgot that."

And she forgot to breathe. In that moment, she sensed that if she made a move, he would stay. And they'd start exploring their feelings for each other.

So she remained still. Patrick opened the door. "I'm late picking up my son."

"Your what?"

He was married? Leave it to her to choose a married guy. No wonder her inner alarm had been clanging with such urgency. Almost a full year in AA, and she still wanted to do things that were bad for her, such as letting Patrick matter.

"My son."

"You're married? I thought you and Raina might be…"

"No," he said with enough emphasis to make it clear he'd denied the suggestion before. "I'm her friend. I'm also divorced." Rage vibrated in his tone. Before she had time to ask why, he reached for the door. "Daphne, this chain is a toy. At least get yourself moved to another room."

"I will." She'd followed like some kid, anxious for a last glance.

Patrick's scent wafted around her. His skin carried a memory of outdoors and spice. Too much aching intimacy had no place between strangers.

He looked at his watch, accidentally exposing the too-fast beat of his pulse in a vein on the underside of his wrist. "I have to get my son," he said again.

She nodded, taking the hint of a second reminder. He was trying to put the boy between them, and she was glad to let him.

He crossed the sidewalk to the parking lot. "You should give Raina a call. She might be right about this place."

Daphne noticed his matter-of-fact tone. Maybe her feelings were coloring the way she looked at him. She knew how to resist. She'd had some problems, a major one with whiskey, but men with eyes like ice and bodies like sin had never been an addiction.

"Thanks for the advice."

A chill April wind blew through the open door. Bits of paper whispered across the parking lot.

Beneath the streetlights, his shiny car stood out from the dull vehicles around it. She pushed her hair out of her eyes, struggling against an insistent need to call him back.

Patrick opened his car door. "Get moved to a different room."

She patted her back pocket for her key card. "Yeah." She shut her door and made a beeline for the window shielded by a smudged curtain and a white sign that dripped the word Office in black.

Only several moments after he'd turned the car in a wide, swift circle, without looking at her, did she move away from her lookout position.

THE NEXT MORNING, the college student on duty behind the counter at Cosmic Grounds came to Daphne's table and passed her a red Sharpie. Smiling shyly, he said, "I found this for you."

"Thanks. I appreciate it." He was already gone, the back of his neck shiny red.

She ducked her head and returned to the classifieds of the *Honesty Sentinel*.

Fortified by a cup of the kid's strongest brew, she started her search. Pickings were slim, but she had to find something she could do. Then she'd worry about coming up with a résumé to impress a prospective employer.

Fifteen minutes later, she'd circled only three jobs that required no experience.

What would Raina think? It all depended on which Raina Daphne met here for coffee—the one who'd sat hunched in the corner of Patrick's office chair, or the one who'd shown up at the coffee shop two days earlier. The second one didn't seem likely to die of shame if her twin took a menial job.

Daphne rested her forehead in one palm and started at the ads again. She could always go back to jury consulting. Considering the mess she'd made of her last case, she could slip by the local jail and set the felons loose on an unsuspecting populace.

Inhaling with all her might, she swallowed hard. The negative stuff was getting too difficult to deal with on her own. She had to find a meeting. It had been over a week since her last one, but the thing they'd drummed into her addled head in rehab had been the importance of always finding an AA meeting.

"I thought I'd find you here. Good thing you keep coming, or they'd be out of business." Raina's voice at her side made Daphne jump.

Daphne set the marker on the table. "Hello, Raina."

Today's perfect outfit was a pink tweed suit and patent-leather pumps.

"Are you on your way to work?" Daphne asked.

"I had a meeting, but I'm planning to look for something like a job."

"Like a job?"

"You know, one that pays." Raina sat across the table. "My mother's health began deteriorating after I finished college, so I helped her keep up with her charity work. We're close to D.C., you know, but we're such a small town in a small county. Our social services don't always stretch to help everyone who needs them." She smoothed her perfect hair. "When Mother couldn't do everything she wanted, I did what she asked."

"That's good work."

"But it was my mother's. Not that I resented being her right hand. I enjoy helping people."

"Who have you been helping? Children?"

"And adults. Anyone who doesn't have a job. Anyone who needs something to eat." She looked away and her uncomfortable expression made Daphne wonder if Raina thought she needed help, too.

"I'm fine. I don't have your kind of money, but I don't need to be rescued."

Raina met her gaze straight on. "I wasn't thinking of you that way. But I knew you'd take it personally." She gripped another steamer trunk-size purse, this one in pale pink that matched her suit. "Remember, I accused you of coming for my money and I refused you before you got a chance to ask."

"That's true." Daphne sipped her coffee. "I guess that proves something."

"That I'm tactless?"

"No. That it's easier to care for people you don't know." Daphne thought about all the people she'd assisted by selecting the juries that freed them. It had been great. She'd thought she was helping the innocent find justice until she'd actually learned the truth about her last client.

"I'd like to help you if you'd let me." Raina flipped her bag open. She pulled out a square opaque plastic container, topped with a blue lid. "To make up for my heavy hand, I'll admit I brought you breakfast. I'm sure they didn't feed you at that hotel."

"Let's ask Patrick if anyone would be foolish enough to eat there," Daphne said without thinking.

"He told me you were upset that I'd sent him."

"Not upset."

"You had every right to be. I don't know why I didn't come myself. Maybe then you'd believe I want you to stay with me."

Her sister's face revealed her regret. Daphne let her qualms go and leaned across the table to touch the container. "You cooked for me?"

"Not exactly." Raina popped the lid. "I didn't make it although I'm an excellent chef. But our cook made an egg casserole with prosciutto and Parmesan this morning—"

"*Our* cook?" Daphne pictured Patrick spooning something from a silver dish across a long table from Raina. Did he and his son live with her?

"Mine now, I guess." Raina's expression tensed and Daphne patted her hand.

"You mean she worked for your mother and you? I'm sorry."

"Who'd you think might be living with me?"

Daphne wasn't about to utter Patrick's name. "No one."

Raina's skin stretched even more tautly across her high cheekbones. "Funny that we're hurting each other even when we don't want to. I'm not seeing Patrick Gannon. He's been my best friend since childhood. His parents were my mother and father's closest friends."

"He says he's divorced."

"And he'll be dealing with Lisa, who's no picnic, until Will is out of college or older."

She took another container from her purse and popped that lid, too, revealing fresh-cut strawberries, blueberries, grapes, pineapple and melon, all very tempting. Daphne licked her lips. She could see how Eve might fall for an apple.

"What's with Patrick and his son?" she asked.

"His ex-wife did horrible things. Bad enough to ensure that she lost custody of Will. He and Patrick are both trying to get over her." Another box held utensils. "She thought I was having an affair with him, too."

"Were you?"

"You're blunt."

"We're getting to know each other."

"I never had an affair with my best friend, who was married and the father of a young son. I have some morals."

"I'm sure you do, but things happen. People are complex."

"Not me. Not that complex." Raina waved at the bowls. "Eat up."

Daphne pulled one closer. "Okay. I'll interrogate you later, but people who say they aren't complex usually are." She studied the containers. "Are you going to share this with me?"

"I already ate. You should take better care of yourself. My mother believed that old adage about breakfast being the most important meal of the day."

"You really do miss her." Daphne's own maternal role models had been so terrifying she'd been glad to escape.

Raina exposed her pain with a brief, sharp nod.

"You're different today," Daphne said. "A mix of yesterday morning and afternoon."

"I didn't know what to expect yesterday. In the morning, I assumed you'd come for the money, but then I was determined to make you stay."

"Make me?"

"I managed, didn't I?" Her smile melted most of the barriers around Daphne's heart. "By last night, I had time to think. I feel a bit awkward this morning. Don't you?"

"Uh-huh."

"Believing that you want to know me, but you don't expect anything else from me seemed gullible, considering."

"But now you trust me? How did you make that change so quickly?"

"I made a start." Raina plucked a strawberry from the box and popped it into her mouth. "And I'm hoping for the best."

"Finally, I see why Patrick is so protective of you."

Raina didn't answer, just looked at her like "What are you saying?"

"You're innocent. An unkind person could take advantage of you."

"Come on. I'm tired of hearing that. I'm as mature as any other woman my age. I've had a life." Raina passed a white brocade napkin. "Did you and Patrick discuss a job?"

Daphne slid the napkin into her lap, anxious that no one else should glimpse it. The food was a delightful surprise—even though bringing one's own food into a café was inappropriate—but the costly linen felt a little too much.

She picked up one of the heavy forks. "There's an A on the handle."

"For Abernathy." Raina reached for the newspaper, scanning the three positions Daphne had circled. "What about the job?"

"I'm not going to work for Patrick. This really is the family silver?"

"We eat with it if that's what you mean." Raina ran her French-manicured index finger around the first ad. "Child minder?" She tapped her cheek. "That's a fancy name for a nanny, you know. For Elena Hennigan and her husband. They want a live-in caregiver for their boys, but they don't say so here because who wants to stay in someone else's home these days? Do you want to live in and take care of toddler boys, aged four and two?"

"I want a job, but little kids make me nervous." What if she only knew how to be the kind of child minder who'd made her younger years a living hell?

"Florist's delivery?" Raina read the next circled item. "You'd find that fun?"

"Fun?" Daphne shook her head. "I need a job. Fun isn't part of the equation."

"But you'd like to enjoy what you do, wouldn't you?" Raina studied her sister. "Do you ever wonder if you might be prejudiced against wealthy, spoiled women?"

Again Daphne admired Raina's ability to laugh at herself. Another surge of affection warmed her.

"I thought of one other thing last night," Raina continued. "I had one paying job." Suddenly fascinated with the blue lid from the silverware box, Raina twirled it with her index finger and thumb. "I wrote papers for other students one term in college. If anyone had ever found out…"

Daphne formed the word *What?* with her lips, but couldn't produce sound. Already, she'd built an image of her sister. Listening while Raina blew it up was like hearing a nuclear explosion. "You—?"

"My father was angry because my grades weren't—" she lifted her head and shook it "—what he expected from an Abernathy. He threatened to cut off my tuition. I had to make money."

"You cheated?" Daphne covered her mouth, but

too late as the guy from the counter leaned in for a closer look.

Raina followed Daphne's eyes. By the time she turned back, her skin was burnished pink. "You never did anything wrong?"

Daphne stared at the breakfast Raina had brought. "Plenty of bad stuff. Probably worse than you can imagine. But I never—"

"Well, now you know I'm not perfect." Raina pushed her chair back. She waved at the plastic on the table. "Just throw that stuff away when you finish."

"I'm not going to throw away your silverware. Raina, wait. Talk to me. I was surprised. I never meant…"

"You didn't like what I said."

She disappeared in a whirl of pink tweed before Daphne could gather up the silverware and damask and plastic and her own bag. Finally, with every-thing in her arms, she ran to the door.

As it closed in her face, she hit the glass, elbows first. Her right funny bone sang a teeth-clenching song.

"Hey," said the kid behind the counter.

Daphne looked at him as she fumbled with the metal handle.

He nodded toward the square outside. "She's mean."

"She isn't." Already, she was protective of Raina, who'd dared to confess one sin. "Leave her alone."

She finally got the door open and peered both ways on the sidewalk. A woman in red was pushing a stroller, and Daphne hopped back to give her room. A guy in a suit that had never touched a rack looked her up and down so deliberately she could almost see herself burying her fist in his stomach. Maybe she had something against rich, spoiled men, too. A little boy sailed his big, green plastic airplane just beneath her chin, roaring an engine noise.

She couldn't see Raina.

"What'd you say to her?"

The kid from the counter had followed. Not much else to do.

She shrugged. "That I was disappointed in her."

"I hate when my dad says that."

She glanced at him. He nodded, wise despite his youth and coffee-stained Cosmic Grounds T-shirt.

"I was the mean one," she told the kid.

She pulled out her phone and dialed Raina's cell number. It rang and rang until voice mail took over. "Raina? I'm sorry. The things I did as a teen you wouldn't believe." Wrong tack. The truth was, she'd been shocked, a little dismayed that Raina's halo had slipped.

Which was ridiculous. Raina would have good reason to board her windows and lock the doors when she finally heard the whole truth about her sister.

"Please, just call me. Trying again might be our best thing. I wouldn't have the courage to ask you if you hadn't come to me in the coffee shop yesterday." She could hardly say her mistake might be a good thing, even though it made her see how much Raina already meant to her. "I think we're starting to be sisters because I seriously need to explain."

CHAPTER FOUR

MITCH ESPY CAME around his desk to take a check from Patrick's hand. Every so often Lisa called Mitch with a request for money. Blackmail. As long as Patrick paid her, she stayed away from Honesty. And Will.

"Don't worry." Mitch laid a hand on Patrick's shoulder. "If Lisa comes back, we'll be ready for her."

"She'll be back. Don't think for a moment she won't. Just come up with a cogent argument for the day she takes us back to court. I'll never allow her to be alone with Will again as long as I live."

Mitch nodded. "I understand, but no judge in his right mind will allow her visitation until she takes care of the problem." He waved the check. "This will keep her at bay a while. It's money she wants."

But Patrick, whose anger at her almost consumed him, didn't believe that someday she wouldn't remember how to love Will again.

"She wants the money for drugs, Mitch. I'm paying to keep her high."

"I can't argue the morals of that again. Will's safety has to come first. Besides, if she could admit she's addicted, she'd be in treatment."

Talking about it—hell, thinking about it—made him too angry to think straight. "Send her the damn check and add the usual note. After she's in treatment, she can get in touch." His skin crawled when he thought how easily she could make her way back to town and into his son's life.

Moments later, he was out on the sidewalk, hurrying toward his office. He still had an arraignment and a deposition to deal with before he picked up Will from his mother's house.

Just then a spring breeze gusted across the square, lifting the hem of a printed, pale orange sundress on the woman seated on a bench. Daphne caught her hem and smoothed it over her crossed knees.

He slowed down. Adjusted his tie. Longed not to care so much that her bare legs looked long and smooth and he could imagine the infinite pleasure of stroking her skin.

"Daphne?"

She looked up, her eyes blank as her mind was obviously elsewhere. But when she recognized him, her body seemed to take over. She sat up straighter, lifting her breasts, tightening the cross of her legs.

"Hey, Patrick."

Her voice was about three octaves huskier than Raina's, and the sweet tones got inside his head.

"What's up?" It wasn't much. It was the best he could manage. "Did you get a new room?"

She looked blank again. "Oh. That." She scooted aside in an unspoken invitation for him to join her. "I got distracted on my way to the office. The lock's fine."

"Are you nuts? You need iron bars, but the chain should at least work. Call the hotel and have them fix it while you're out."

Her smile mocked his naiveté. "You saw the place. I'm not sure that guy at the desk could unfasten his a—himself from the seat of his chair. He's certainly not up to installing hardware."

"Either change rooms, have him fix it, or I'll come fix it."

She stared at him.

"Most women would think I'm overstepping," he said.

"Uh-huh."

They stared at each other, and it was like drinking his fill when he was dying of thirst. Finally, he had to look away.

"Why do you care?" she asked.

Good question. One that had kept him awake for the two nights since he'd last seen her.

"Put it down to an urge to run my own patriarchal society. I look after your sister. I'm my mother's financial adviser. For my ex-wife…" He'd nursed Lisa for years, thinking she was on the verge of death. "I'm tired of being responsible, but it's a hard habit to break."

"Okay. Don't worry."

"I will if you don't get it fixed."

"I can use a screwdriver as well as the guy in the office." She lifted the paper he hadn't noticed on her lap. "I'm looking for a job. Do you know a Mrs. Hennigan? She's so desperate for child care she offered me the chance to look after her boys."

"Did you accept it?"

"I saw her son Tyler riding their beagle. Tyler's two, and the beagle must be about eighty-two. I figured I'd have to report Tyler to the SPCA, and that wouldn't win me any points with his mommy."

"What about the older one? Drake?"

"He hit me with a spitball in the back of the head before I could escape the house. Mrs. Hennigan says the boys are having separation anxiety since their last nanny left. I'm betting they could find her in the nearest home for child-care providers driven crazy by their charges."

"What did you do before you came here?"

"Whatever."

Oh, yeah. He'd already tried that.

"You weren't boosting cars?"

"I'm not sure you're joking."

The suggestion seemed to spook him. "Why?" He shook his head. "Raina was right. I could find something for you in my office."

"Don't tempt me." She pleated her skirt with her fingers, then added, "I upset Raina."

He tugged at his collar, not wanting to know. "Yeah?" The arraignment, the deposition, his son's fears, as well as Will's longing for his mother, all had a place in line for Patrick's attention. He had enough to do. Walking away from both Raina and Daphne would be the smartest thing to do. "What happened?"

"She told me something." Daphne scooped her hair behind her ear. "I was shocked, and she got upset."

"How could Raina shock you?"

Daphne twisted her mouth. "I'm not sure I can say."

"Did you talk it out with her?"

"She walked out. I ran after her, but I couldn't find her." She went back to ironing her skirt with her index finger and thumb. "I've tried calling her, but she doesn't answer. Is she good at holding grudges?"

"I can't remember her ever holding one. Maybe if you gave me a little more to go on. Was this serious? Do you want me to talk to her?"

Daphne's spontaneous laugh warmed him like the spring sun at his back. "I think I can handle apologizing myself. If she'll answer her phone."

"You matter to her," he said. "Once you're more at ease with each other, you'll be able to argue and make up like normal sisters."

"You know this because?"

"I've known Raina all her life."

"You belong here," she said, and it wasn't a platitude. "And my sister belongs here. I've never been in a place where people belonged like they do here." She touched his arm, startling him. "You play your parts, and you know what to expect. I like the safety of that."

"Are you looking for safety, Daphne?"

She met his gaze, and then hers fell to his mouth. Wanting her was crazy. It made his blood rush so that he actually felt dizzy.

He leaned closer. Around him, all sound seemed to magnify, children's voices and birds singing. The seesaw scraping over metal. New leaves fluttering on the trees.

The sun seemed hotter. Daphne's perfume imprinted itself on his senses, and yet he couldn't get enough.

"What are you doing?" she asked so close he almost imagined their lips touched.

"Making a big mistake," he said. "You know about my son?"

"I know you've had problems."

"With my ex-wife. Will needs me." He stared at her mouth, wondering if he'd ever forget the lush sweet lines of her lips, begging to be tasted, taken, enjoyed. "Will needs all of me."

It wasn't what he'd meant to say. Will and he needed each other to heal, but he couldn't explain that. He could barely put words together. He hadn't touched a woman in so long, and he wanted this woman more than he could believe.

She leaned back. He felt the loss of her. She'd been so close to moving into his arms. Then she stood, smoothing her skirt with trembling hands that he wanted to take and hold. He wanted to pull her close to him.

"I have an appointment with a flower lady on the other side of the courthouse." Daphne tossed the paper over him, letting it sail into the mesh wastebasket.

"Wait." He caught her arm. The small bones beneath her skin made him loosen his grip. Though she tried to be tough, she couldn't hide her fragility. "Do you want me to call Raina?"

Softness in her eyes nearly undid him. "Thank you, but I don't need you to help me with Raina. I believe she'll try again with me."

"I'd like to help."

She nodded with a pointed glance at his hand still engulfing her wrist. "I'm not used to having a man take care of things for me."

"Never in your life?" he asked, as if he knew it to be true. Somehow, he did. He understood the foster-care system, and he saw evidence of its worst failures in her overly developed sense of independence.

Twenty-eight years of living virtually alone, and yet she'd reached out to him and to Raina with no promise of acceptance.

"It's time you knew the truth about Honesty. Taking care is what small towns do best." He let her go, but she rubbed her forearm.

"I know you're trying to make me feel welcome. Especially after what happened in your office, I appreciate that you actually care."

Care? He was trying not to care too much.

As she walked away, another gust pushed her dark hair over her shoulder. She glanced back, as if drawn. She couldn't look away, either.

He felt a strange jolt of happiness. It might be hope.

DAPHNE STOPPED on the other side of the square and dropped onto the first bench out of Patrick Gannon's sight. She couldn't let him distract her. Her sister was her priority. They needed to settle their disagreement now.

She opened her phone and searched the record of her incoming calls until she found her twin's phone number. Then she pushed talk and willed Raina to answer. She didn't.

"Raina," she spoke softly, aware of couples and families strolling past in the spring sun. Raina wouldn't want her airing their dirty laundry over the phone. "Please call me back. I need to tell you why I had no right to—think or say anything about what you told me."

Hell, she'd stolen newspapers to layer between her clothes. And food when her hands were shaking so hard from hunger she couldn't understand why she wasn't caught. Once she'd pilfered a romance novel from a drugstore's Dumpster and then protected the book as if it were a window into a world she'd never be allowed to visit.

One stormy night, huddling beneath a thick piece of cardboard and an overpass, she'd shoved the book beneath her sweatshirt to keep it safe.

She wanted to tell Raina, to explain why she'd put her sister on a pedestal. But not over the phone. They had a hard enough time understanding each other face-to-face. She'd confess all her sins in person, but for now, Daphne closed her phone.

The time flashed across its black screen. She had to make her interview. She stood, straightening her secondhand cardigan. At the far corner on this side of the square, Miriam Burke, proprietress of Bundle of Blooms, was hoping for a viable candidate to deliver her flowers.

Daphne advanced on the store with all the confidence of a night-blooming orchid. She'd better look as if she'd be good at this.

Someone had arranged bright spring bouquets and sheaves of fresh-cut flowers in the two large windows that flanked a green door decoupaged in ribbon and posies.

Daphne glanced down the street, unwilling to admit, even to herself, that she was hoping to see Patrick's tall, broad back, the confident jut of his shoulders among the citizens milling around Honesty's square.

Damn him for getting into her head like this.

She looked everywhere but at herself in the reflective windows. She licked her lips. Her mouth felt so damn dry when she stressed. It might be a nothing job to Raina, but Daphne had to find a way to pay the rent.

She also had to find a meeting. Missing another one was asking for trouble.

Her phone rang as she reached for the doorknob. She pulled it out of her pocket. Raina's name on the caller ID made her thumb edge toward the talk button, but that conversation would take more than two and a half minutes, which was when she was scheduled to meet Miriam Burke.

She eased the door open. A woman barely older than Daphne looked up from a huge crystal vase half filled with roses and carnations. The rest of the flowers were lined up on green paper along the counter.

"Hello." Daphne held out her hand. She should have wiped her palm.

"You must be Daphne Soder." While the woman

shook her hand, she stared as if Daphne's face were a science project. "But you look exactly like someone I know."

On the verge of explaining, Daphne stopped. Raina might not want her revealing their relationship. An eggbeater took a quick stir at her innards, and Daphne smiled and let it go.

"Yes. I'm Daphne."

"We spoke on the phone. I'm Miriam Burke. Do you mind if I finish?"

"Go ahead. I'll enjoy watching."

Miriam flashed a quick smile. She continued placing greenery and stems until she stood back with a last rose. In it went, and the arrangement looked perfect.

"Did you always know how to do that?" Daphne asked. "Or can it be learned?"

"Would you like to learn?"

"I think so."

"Good." Miriam wrapped up the scraps, dumped the paper and cuttings in a bucket and then eased the vase to a safe corner on the counter. "Did you bring a résumé?"

"I did." It contained nothing that made her a sure bet for a florist's shop, but she'd worked hard during college and after. And she'd had some retail experience.

Nevertheless, she took the envelope from her purse and slid it onto the counter. Miriam took out the pages and scanned them.

"You're a jury consultant. Why would you want to work here?"

"I haven't worked as a jury consultant for eighteen months."

"Why?"

She'd always ducked that question. Did it need to be asked for this kind of job? "It wasn't a good fit. As you can see, I've done retail work, and I've had a variety of positions so I can learn new skills."

"I'm not suggesting you need the criminology degree." She glanced at the résumé again. "But the variety of jobs you've held makes me wonder if you'd stay long enough to be worth my while."

Everyone in this town was as blunt as a sledgehammer. "Yes," Daphne said, and she had no trouble meeting Miriam's pale blue eyes because she was telling the truth. "I'll be here." She'd alienated her sister, but Honesty was home unless Raina refused to see her again.

"When did you move here?"

"A few days ago."

Miriam's mouth twisted. Those jury consultant skills hadn't entirely deserted Daphne. She'd learned good instincts about people in ugly situations, and she could read Miriam's doubts.

"I'm not drifting," she said. "I plan to stay."

Her résumé seemed to require all of Miriam's concentration. Translation, she was considering taking the leap.

"Your interest in staying in Honesty has something to do with the way you look?"

Daphne touched her own cheek. "Maybe I love the idea of a small town."

"Okay." Miriam's smile was knowing, but she went on without pushing for more information about Daphne's resemblance to Raina. "Most newcomers your age come bearing the requisite two-point-some-thing children and a puppy."

"And a spouse." The town was too picture perfect to go without.

"The spouse is not always required." Miriam shrugged. "I'm looking for someone with a driver's license, and I get that you don't want to share your personal business."

"I just want a change." The lie came easily.

Miriam eyed her with continued indecision. "You can't be worse than the high-school kids who've dumped me for a pep rally or a debate-team weekend."

"Debate team?"

"I know. That's as hard to believe as you wanting this job." Miriam's smile flashed. "It looks good on college apps. Shows they're critical thinkers."

"Wow. A plan in high school." Other than escaping foster care, she'd had none.

Miriam moved down the counter to pat a huge, hunching gray machine. "This is my cash register. It's old. I bought it secondhand, and it has a few quirks."

Just like that, Daphne found herself employed. Miriam took her through the refrigerators where she stored flowers she ordered from out-of-town suppliers. She was more excited about the small green-house at the back.

"After I built this, I couldn't afford a state-of-the-art cash register, but I have live plants, and I get to play whenever I want. I love it."

"I envy your passion." She'd loved being excited that way when certain cases came to trial.

"I breed roses." Miriam leaned down to cradle a rose's fleshy petals. "Of course, everyone wants to create a new rose. I'm a cliché." She spun toward the shop. "Come back inside. We'll go through today's orders."

Daphne followed her, distracted by the courthouse spire that towered crookedly in the glass-paned roof. "I've never seen a greenhouse attached to a florist's before."

"Did you notice the shopping area behind us?" Miriam didn't wait for an answer. "It's pedestrian only, which put my parking spots out of reach. Instead of leaving the area empty, I built the greenhouse and we have to depend on the parking out front."

"Does it hurt·business?" Daphne asked.

"You mean will I be able to afford you? If you're agreeable to the salary I can offer, we'll do fine." She stroked the petals of an orchid that seemed to preen beneath her fingers. "I know the ad said I wanted delivery only, but that was when I thought I'd be settling for a kid. If you want to work in the shop, too, I might add something to your paycheck. You may not be using any of your training, but you've obviously got what it takes to stick with something."

"Thanks."

Again, Miriam grinned as they made their way back to the shop. From behind the counter, Miriam drew out an apron of poppies and blue crocuses printed on a white cotton background. She offered it to Daphne. "You want to stay the rest of today?"

Daphne hesitated. She owed Raina that call. "Okay." After all, she also had to pay rent for her scary hotel-room-by-the-month.

CHAPTER FIVE

"COURT IS ADJOURNED. I'll see both attorneys in my chambers tomorrow morning at eight. The jury reports on Monday morning at nine. I know tomorrow is Saturday," Judge Masters went on, "but I'd like a brief word with both counselors."

"What's that about?" Alexis Long was Patrick's second chair. She watched the judge depart.

Patrick was already stuffing papers and a legal pad into his briefcase. He lowered his voice, mindful of their client, who was talking with his daughter. "Probably wants to suggest we persuade our client to not contest the charge of attacking his wife, then Masters will massage the prosecutor into suggesting a fair sentence."

Alexis touched his sleeve. "Go get Will." She gestured to the rest of the books and notepads. "Take what you need in case you're right about what he wants, and I'll get everything else back to the office."

Her offer tempted him, but he always left first. "You work as hard as I do, and I take advantage of you every time court runs late."

"I'm going home to a cat." She picked up one of the notepads. "And even he won't miss me until his dinner's late. Will needs you." Alexis was kind considering the dark circles under her eyes.

How much did she know? How much did everyone know, despite his best efforts to keep Will safe from gossip? "You're tired, too," he said.

"I'm not a kid who needs his dad's attention."

"You sure?" he asked.

"Positive." She nudged him with her elbow and he needed no further invitation to dump everything and run. "Don't worry. This case will end soon either way."

She glanced at their client, Hal Baker. Patrick and Alexis were using every weapon in their legal arsenal to defend the man, but Patrick had come to doubt Hal's innocence.

He gave Hal a level look. Even in repose, listening to his daughter, the only person who still had any faith in him, the man's ruddy face revealed his anger.

Patrick hated to lose a case, but this time it might be for the best. He'd tried to talk Hal into therapy, but the man refused, even when Alexis and Patrick argued it might keep him out of jail.

Alexis reached around Patrick for a book. "Forget about Hal for tonight. I'll talk to him about trying to look a little less—enraged." She pressed Patrick's briefcase into his hands and urged him toward the aisle. "Don't make Will wait."

"Thanks." He wished he could promise the bad days with his son would be over soon, too, but considering Will's poor sleep last night and his tantrums at lunch today, that didn't seem likely.

With a sense of foreboding, Patrick drove past his own Federal-style row house on his way to the new neighborhood just beyond Honesty's city limits where his mother lived. He had to stop at an electronic gate and punch in her security code.

Gloria Gannon had fled to her mini-mansion soon after Patrick's father died from a massive heart attack. She claimed the wide-open rooms and the smell of brand-new paint and drywall had seduced her after fifty-two years in the row house, but Patrick wondered if she was running from memories of happiness.

He followed a winding road through the "estates" to the faux-Tudor manse she'd made her home. Funny how he yearned to make the kind of memories that had left his mother stalking the halls of their family home night and day, unable to sleep.

He parked in the circular driveway and rang the bell that clanged, echo after echo. Half the double wooden door opened slowly.

His five-year-old son had only so much muscle weight. He was already giggling when he brushed his dark brown hair out of his eyes. Happy eyes, not filled with fear and betrayal.

Relief turned to joy as Patrick reached for his boy.

"Hi, Daddy." Will let go of the iron door handle and flew at Patrick, half hug, half attack. "I thought you weren't coming."

Will had him by the throat every time he got

scared. "I'll always come, buddy." He beamed into his son's eyes, determined to make Will believe. "You're never going to look for me and not find me."

Patrick's mother came to the door behind Will, her hands fluttering. She was tough. She could run the world, starting with the causes she loved best in Honesty, but she'd thrown everything aside for Will. "I told him not to worry."

She'd refused to let Patrick hire a younger baby-sitter, and he had to believe she was right about family being best for his little guy. "You could have called again if you were still worried, Will." He scooped up his son, who held on for dear life.

"We tried to call again. I left you a boy snail message."

"But you don't like boy snail," Patrick said, grinning.

"Voice mail," Gloria said while Patrick laughed. "It's voice mail, Will. Someone will mock him one day, son, if you don't correct him."

"I don't like boy snail. You should answer your phone when I call, Daddy. It took you too long to call back."

"I was in court." He twisted the phone on his belt so he could see its face. The black screen was black all over. "Or my battery's dead. Sorry, Mom." He pressed his son's wriggling body into his chest. "But you're okay. You didn't need me after all."

Will had woken from a short nap, thinking he was in Lisa's car outside the dress shop where she'd overdosed the last day she'd ever been alone with him. Patrick had managed to duck into a stall in the courthouse bathroom earlier in the afternoon to reassure his son.

"Grandma said I was okay, too. She said I'd never have to go in a cold car again."

"Never," Patrick said, refusing to give in to the fear he might be wrong. "What else did you do this afternoon?" he asked.

His mother took over. "We made rolls. Kneading is good for little boys as well as grandmas. Good heavens, I've left you standing on the stoop. Come in and have dinner, son. We saved you some."

"I can't." Even though his stomach growled loud enough to make Will work his way to the floor where he could point and laugh. "It's already late, and this little jokester needs a shower before bed. I have to see Judge Masters in the morning. Can you watch him again?" He hated asking. A teacher workday had altered Will's schedule, and two days in a row with his grandmother—much as he loved her—was a break in routine for the child.

"I'm glad to as long as you can get to your phone."

Where other little boys thrived on surprises and late nights for fun, his son needed everything to happen just as it was supposed to. Dinner, shower, bedtime story, night-light on and then "Good night, Daddy." Who knew if the boy would ever say goodnight to his mother again?

No. Will had had a nightmare today, but that didn't mean tomorrow would bring more bad memories.

"I'll have the phone, and Will knows he's safe with us. Don't you, big guy?"

"Yeah, yeah, but I'm a little hungry, too." Will rubbed his belly and Gloria turned to hurry back to the kitchen.

"Let me put some rolls in a bag for you. You can come inside long enough to take them?"

"Daddy, I can't leave without my bread."

"Okay, buddy." Will sounded almost like himself. When the small things mattered, they were on even ground. Just inside the wide foyer, Patrick found Will's jacket on a bench. "We'll get you ready to go while Grandma brings your stuff."

He set Will on the bench. Will swung his feet as if nothing at all had happened today. Except a tear-shaped spot of dirt smudged his cheekbone. Patrick licked his finger and wiped it off.

"Dad, no spit."

"Your shoes aren't tied, buddy."

"I can do it." He tied the laces with ultimate concentration and then lifted his hands like a rodeo star who'd just roped a bull. "Now you do my jacket."

"Did you have fun with Grandma today?"

"Yeah, but I thought I was in Mommy's car."

"I remember."

"Did you get mad when we called you that first time?"

"Are you kidding? I always want to talk to you, and when you feel bad, you should call me as quick as you can." Even Judge Masters had understood. Only Hal had grown impatient.

"I love you, Daddy."

"I love you, too." He hugged Will as close as he could get him. "Are you still trying to stop being afraid?"

He moved his head up and down with so much emphasis, it was surprising he didn't crack a vertebra. "I'm not always scared. Just when I memember."

"Me, too, so you just let me be scared, and you forget about it." Patrick would never forget that Will could have died if that early-winter day had been colder. The snow had started climbing up the rear window when the lady who owned the shop next door had come out to sweep her sidewalk. While beating her broom against the curb, she'd spied Will, leaning into the back window, almost asleep.

"You're still mad at Mommy."

"Not mad." Enraged, murderous. Panicked that she might ever get her hands on his child again. But none of that mattered right now if Will was okay. "Let's think about happier things."

"I miss her," Will said.

Patrick forced his mouth into a smile. He'd do anything to make life easier for Will. "I know you do. She'll probably call you soon."

"I hope so." He jumped off the bench as his grandmother came down the hall, holding out three containers.

"I made chowder. It's perfect with the rolls, and I put together a little salad. Don't complain it's too much. I put in a little extra so Will could have seconds."

"Thanks, Mom." His stomach growled again, and

Will poked him. He tried to corral his son's hand. "I'm not sure when I last ate. Hey, you, with the pointy finger—give Grandma a kiss and let's go home."

Will jumped into his grandmother's arms. She staggered backward, laughing, and covered his face in kisses. "I'll be at the door in the morning the second the bell rings," she said.

"Can we make something to eat again?" Will pounded the heel of his shoe on the floor, as if he was testing his own strength. "I like cookies a lot, Grandma."

"Me, too. We'll talk about what kind we both like in the morning." She glanced over his head at Patrick, who just smiled.

"Baking cookies with Grandma sounds great, Mom. Thanks." He lifted the packages. "Ready, bud?"

"Wait. I wanted to tell you—ask you." Gloria glanced down at her grandson, who'd run to dangle off Patrick's arm. "I heard a funny thing when we stopped to buy tomatoes at the co-op today. Raina—apparently she's changed her style. Going for a younger look, Mrs. Bergstrom says."

"Younger look?"

"You know, sundress, messy hair, instead of something from her dress-for-success designer closet. She's all right, isn't she? I worry about her since Hannah…"

Hannah had been his mother's best friend. "She's fine. You must be talking about Daphne, her sister."

"Sister?" His mother treated him to her infamous

let-me-count-your-brain-cells look. "What are you talking about?"

Will chose that moment to fall off Patrick's sleeve, landing on the polished floor with a thud and a grunt.

"I'll call you, Mother." He adjusted the stack of containers, holding one beneath his chin, while he leaned sideways to help his son up.

His mother scooped Will back to his feet. "You're okay, sweetheart," she said in the way of caregivers. "Patrick, you must stay and tell me what's going on."

"I can't." For one thing, she had the eyes of a born private detective, and although he hardly knew Daphne, he had plenty to hide where she was concerned. "You can talk to Raina about it, but it turns out her parents kept a big secret from her."

"Hannah and Lars gave up a—" She covered her mouth. The last thing Will needed to hear was that anyone had given up any child at any time. She glanced at him. "I won't believe it."

"They didn't, but Raina can tell you more." Patrick nudged Will toward the door. "Let me have your backpack, buddy." He took the green bag off his son's shoulders. "Actually, if I were you, Mother, I'd wait for Raina to bring up the subject."

"Mmm, hmm," his mother said. She moved ahead of them to the door and leaned against the jamb. "Love you both."

"Bye, Grandma. See you tomorrow."

He managed to get out of her house without saying anything more about Daphne or revealing the strange, but overpowering, effect she had on him.

Gloria shut the door and Will scampered down the steps, pausing to leap onto the cobbled driveway with a superhero flourish.

Without warning, Patrick saw Daphne's face. Smiling, with pure temptation in her eyes. Why hadn't he kissed her in the park? A kiss was no commitment. It might be a test.

"Dad? Unlock the doors."

Coming to his senses, he used the keyless entry and then opened the backdoor to help Will into his booster seat. He set his mother's containers on the car's floor.

"I'm hungry, Daddy. Can I have a bread while you drive?"

Patrick checked the belts. "Did you eat a good lunch?"

"Grandma said I did. I promise I won't get crumbs on the seat."

Hell, his car was more like a lunch wagon these days. He took out a roll and his stomach rumbled again, sending Will into another storm of laughter.

"Mmm, it's good, Daddy." He pinched off a piece and held it out. "Try some."

Patrick popped it into his mouth. "Wow, that's good, buddy."

"Mmm, hmm. Let's sing about the bus, Dad."

"I'm chewing."

"Okay. The wheels on the bus… The wheels…" He flung his feet. "Come on, Dad. Sing, too."

Patrick pushed his homemade roll into his cheek and slurred along until they finished. "I'm glad you taught me this song, son."

"You can chew for a minute. Do you know 'Bingo,' Dad?"

DAPHNE OPENED her car's trunk. She'd packed a couple of the arrangements in cardboard boxes to keep them from tipping over, and Miriam had asked her to bring the boxes back.

"I'll help you." Miriam startled her, walking up from behind. "Sorry," she said. "I saw you drive up. Did you have any problems?"

"No. Everyone was home." She stacked the boxes. "This is a pretty cool job. Everyone's so glad to see me."

"Anyone offer a tip?"

"No." Miriam had asked her not to take them. "And I'd heard small towns are generous." She lifted the boxes and shut the trunk as a greenish-silver SUV drove past. "But they sure are small."

"What's small?" Miriam followed her gaze.

"Towns. I keep seeing the same faces." Even driving a gas-guzzling SUV, Patrick looked good to her. He'd glanced into the rearview mirror as he'd driven past, his mouth moving as if he was—singing.

"Oh, that's Patrick Gannon. He lives just beyond the shopping area I showed you. You know him?" Miriam took the boxes.

"I met him briefly." Daphne was deliberately

casual. "Was that his son in the backseat?" She'd seen a tiny head moving back and forth.

"You know about that, too?" Miriam looked embarrassed. "Sorry. You know the other thing about small towns? Gossip. Also a cliché, but some clichés are based in reality."

"I'm asking too many questions." Patrick had her so mixed up she was snooping into his personal life with the first objective person she met. "I'm sorry, Miriam."

Miriam hugged the boxes close. "It's all right. Someone else will tell you if I don't. And Patrick doesn't talk to anyone since his ex left town about six months ago."

Her first reaction was sympathy for what he must be going through. Her second was a realization that he probably wouldn't be willing to trust any woman. So letting herself fall for him was another step down the wrong road.

To hell with the fact that she'd never felt such an intense attraction before. It came with a man focused on his son's needs and his ex's departure.

"I shouldn't have asked. I'd rather not be part of a small-town cliché." Daphne grabbed the rest of the boxes and headed back inside the shop.

"I understand you're curious." Miriam set her boxes in the storeroom and then took Daphne's from her arms. She looked at Daphne's mostly clean apron. "Well, we're finished. Did you enjoy your first day?"

Daphne's grin felt forced. She was upset with herself at letting her feelings for Patrick get in the way of her priorities. "It's been great, even better than I expected."

Miriam held out her hand. "Lucky for both of us, you answered my ad."

They shook, and Daphne felt her first sense of belonging. "I'll help you sweep up before I go."

"Yeah? Thanks." Miriam opened a cupboard behind the big fridges and pulled out two brooms. She passed one to Daphne. "You take the floor in here, and I'll do the greenhouse. You can leave after you finish. I want to repot a few plants."

"See you tomorrow."

"Great."

Smiling, Daphne swept, listening to Miriam's ballet slippers whisper down the hardwood floor.

Her smile only wavered as she remembered she'd been hoping Raina would be the one to welcome her to Honesty.

After she dumped the dustpan and put away the broom, she went into Miriam's office. There was no phone book in the hotel room. She found Miriam's in a desk drawer without—thank God—stumbling onto anything personal.

Daphne leafed through the Yellow Pages, keeping an eye on the door to the hall. She might be willing to share some confidences with Miriam, but some secrets she'd just as soon keep from the woman who'd eventually sign her paychecks.

She found what she was looking for, jotted the information down on her palm and then placed the phone book back inside the drawer. In the hall, she turned toward the greenhouse.

"Do you want me to lock the door?"

A faint "thanks" floated back. Daphne set the lock before she went out and got into her car. Traffic was lighter as the streets grew dark.

She drove around the square until she found the church listed in the Yellow Pages. The side door stood open. Another welcome, though not the kind a lot of the folks who usually attended services here might even know about.

Daphne parked and got out of her car. Nightfall had brought a chill to the air. Her sweater proved little protection.

As she started inside, a woman came down the side staircase, tucking a leather notebook beneath her elbow. Daphne looked up to ask if she knew where the meeting was being held.

Again, she peered into a mirror of her own face. Again, the shock was physical.

"Daphne? How did you know—" A smile had started forming, but it froze on Raina's face.

"I didn't." With a familiar sense of desperation, she looked for the right door to escape through. She needed the support of a meeting tonight as much as she ever had.

"You're not looking for me?"

"Not right this minute, but we need to talk." She'd come prepared to tell a roomful of alcoholics that she was one of them, but this was no way to tell her sister.

Raina looked down the stairs. "I don't understand."

"I looked this place up in the phone book."

"There's no service tonight. Where are you going

at this hour?" She checked her watch to make sure she had the time right. Her notebook slipped.

Daphne grabbed it and handed it over. "There's a meeting in this building."

Raina glanced downward again. "Oh." She stared at Daphne, her eyes troubled.

"Maybe we should talk now."

"No." Raina took one step backward, and Daphne felt the rejection with the force of a slap to the face.

Tears started to her eyes. "I'm taking care of my problem," she said, unwilling to let her sister see how much her reaction hurt.

"I'm sorry."

"Don't worry about it." It was the last thing she meant, but she had pride. "I'm fine."

"You're not and neither am I. We're both too quick to misunderstand."

Raina came down a step, and Daphne wanted nothing more than to be the one to back away this time. But you didn't change your life making the same old mistakes.

"Come to my house. After." She took one last look toward the stairs. "The meeting's down there."

"After is too late for tonight." And she wasn't sure she could face Raina with her best intentions intact.

"Tomorrow, then."

"Okay, but it'll have to be late in the day. I have a job."

Raina looked up, her eyes wide and far more innocent than the ones Daphne saw in her own mirror.

"Which one did you take?"

Daphne laughed. "At least you assumed I'd have the choice. I'm working for Miriam Burke, the florist. Delivering flowers."

"I'm so sorry about this, Daphne."

"Forget it," Daphne said, recognizing that the kindness in Raina's voice meant she could, as well. "I want to explain, but we'll talk tomorrow."

"Do you know where I live?"

"No," she said with a start of surprise.

Raina pulled an envelope out of her purse and then rummaged for a pen. She scrawled words on the envelope and passed it across. "I'll find something for us to eat."

Daphne nodded, too uneasy to contemplate food. "Okay, but Raina, it's not as bad as you might be expecting."

"I believe you."

Raina took Daphne's hand. Daphne hung on, imagining she could feel her twin's pulse. The tears were going to rain like a tropical storm if she didn't get out of here.

She pulled Raina close and hugged her, briefly enough that Raina could put it down as a small collision.

"Thanks, Raina. You can't know what that means."

She barely touched any of the stairs on her way down. A sign posted on the third door she came to gave her almost as much relief as her first-ever double shot of Glenfiddich.

She eased inside just as another woman latched

both hands around the bull-nosed edges of the podium at the front of the room.

Here was safety and a reminder that she was the kind of woman a sister could love. She'd fought her worst instincts to become a good woman. And Raina believed in her. That had to mean her effort was not in vain.

The woman at the podium waited with a smile for Daphne to take the first open chair. "My name is Camille," she said, "and I'm an alcoholic."

"Hello, Camille," Daphne said with the others.

CHAPTER SIX

WHEN RAINA FINALLY picked up the receiver, Daphne almost sang with happiness.

But then Raina spoke. "I'm sorry I've been so out of pocket. I've had a busy week, several meetings, some loose ends to tie up from my mother's work."

The voice didn't even sound like Raina's, and Daphne could find no response. In the nine days since she'd seen her sister in the church, Raina had kept putting off the talk they needed to have. Her compassion seemed to have been instinctual, but premature.

"Daphne?"

"I'm digging for the courage to ask the obvious question."

"What are you talking about?"

"Maybe you don't want to talk now that you know I'm an alcoholic."

"Where do you get these ideas?" Raina must be moving around. A door squeaked on her side of the conversation. "Give me a sec." A few footsteps—heels on marble—and then she seemed to push through another squeaking door. "I sounded so stiff because I felt ridiculous saying I had engagements and commitments when you're working at a florist's."

"I assume you're not being condescending?"

"Of course not. But your situation is making me very aware of mine. I was sitting at a conference table yesterday, eating foie gras while we decided how many blankets a shelter down near your hotel needs."

"You waste money on foie gras while people are sleeping cold in the street?"

"Don't make me think about it any harder. I feel ridiculous talking about my stuff when you do real work." She lifted her voice. "But I did tell them we needed to eat pb and j from now on, like the clients who use the facilities."

"Clients?"

"Give me a little bit of understanding."

Daphne changed the subject. "When do you want to meet?"

"Tonight would be great if you can make it."

They agreed on a time, and Daphne told herself to take Raina at her word and stop borrowing trouble. She shut her phone and entered the shop to find a crowd, several layers deep.

Of course. It was the day before Mother's Day. Miriam had put up posters and advertisements before Daphne had even started at the shop, but Daphne hadn't connected Mother's Day with Raina's loss until now.

On the day before her first Mother's Day alone, she'd be celebrating by hearing the tale of her sister's ugly past.

Miriam hurtled out of the back, peering over the

heads of three customers. "Remember how we dis-cussed your working in the shop, too?"

Daphne went to the counter, already reaching for an apron.

The morning sped by. She had no talent for ar-ranging, but she could gather the stems and blooms Miriam wanted. She sold most of the arrangements waiting in the refrigerators.

"Talk about trial by fire," Miriam said a little after noon as she took over a bow Daphne had manhan-dled into tattered ugliness. She tossed Daphne's bow into the waste can and cut a new length of ribbon. "I'll get this." As someone else opened the door, she pressed her hands and the ribbon to her ears. "That bell is driving me crazy."

"I'll see to them." Wiping her hands on her apron, Daphne watched Miriam replace the mess she'd made.

"Don't worry." Miriam glanced over her shoulder. "It's a matter of practice."

Daphne went to the front, and almost collided with Patrick, studying the meager selection of bouquets still arranged in one of the refrigerators.

Seeing him so unexpectedly was more than star-tling. "Hi," she said, her voice squeaky because her throat had tightened. He was wearing a dark suit and a white shirt. Office uniform for billions of men every day. But Daphne had to fight to keep from sliding her hand over his chest, searching for the flat stomach muscles beneath his expensive cotton shirt.

"Hi." He didn't turn to her. His hard-edged profile presented a challenge. She willed him to look at her.

She wanted to see whether his need was as compelling as hers.

"May I help you?"

Her stiff tone did the trick. She expected ice in his eyes, but he turned as if he'd been waiting to meet her gaze. His eyes devoured her as she tucked her hands behind her back to keep from touching him.

"Daphne," he said.

She nodded.

He came closer. "I heard you'd found this job."

"I was worried you and Raina might disapprove."

"Work's important," he said. "I have clients who—" He stopped, his smile, self-mocking and irresistible. "Not that I'm comparing you to my clients."

He probably could. She'd done things that would shock him as much—maybe more than—Raina. The knowledge restored Daphne to reality.

"You need something for Mother's Day?"

"My son wants a bouquet, or maybe a plant for his mother for tomorrow. I need to look at your catalog. Can you still deliver an arrangement today?"

"Sure." She came around the counter, looking for a boy, but Patrick was alone. "Where is your son?"

"He's at home with my mother. I promised to bring a picture of whatever I send."

She led him to the catalog on a stand on the counter. "I can make a copy."

"What do you think?" Patrick asked. "Carnations?"

"Does your son have a favorite color?"

"Orange, and Lisa likes carnations."

She tried to believe her stab of envy had nothing

to do with Patrick. She wanted to be a woman whose tastes were remembered.

"I saw an arrangement with orange-tipped ones." She leafed through the plastic-sleeved pages. "Here we are. You have three options."

"Will would choose the big one."

Daphne laughed and looked up to find Patrick watching her. His intensity literally robbed her of oxygen.

They weren't alone. Suddenly, she felt as if everyone else in the shop was also waiting, breath held, to see what happened next. But no one else could be as aware of the line of his chin, the dark shadow of his beard, the contrast between rough and smooth of his hand on her wrist and his mouth, curved in a tense invitation.

She longed to move close to him, to let his mouth persuade her that nothing was wrong about her unexpected need of him.

Instead, she made herself remember her job. "Do you have an address?"

At first he looked blank. His fingers, long, strong, capable, trembled as he fished a folded piece of paper from an inside pocket. She caught a whiff of his spicy scent as he leaned toward her, smoothing the paper open. "She'll receive it by tomorrow?"

"As long as we send it by five." She glanced at the wide-faced, Victorian clock over the door. "You still have plenty of time."

She entered Lisa Gannon's information, but it was like typing with a set of ten cucumbers. Her hands didn't want to work. Finally, she got as far as taking Patrick's credit card and running it through Miriam's old-fashioned machine.

He signed the charge slip. She pushed his copy to him.

"Thanks." He took it from her.

Their fingertips brushed. Just like a heroine in a romance novel, she felt a surge of desire. Yearning that made her stomach feel hollow and her legs heavy.

"Let me make a copy of the picture of the bouquet." She took the sheet out and ran it through the copier and pushed that across the counter, too.

He folded it and added it to the same pocket as his ex-wife's address. "I want to see you," he said, low-voiced.

She studied the other customers. No one seemed to be as interested as she feared. "Call me," she said. "Or come to the hote—no, I don't want you to come there."

"I'm not a snob."

"I'm not sure this is even the right conversation to be having."

"We have to," he said in an almost-resigned tone. "I can't pretend I don't—" He glanced at the others in the store now. "It's too strong," he said. "We can't pretend nothing's happening between us."

"Patrick, I'm working," she said, willing him to leave, yet wanting him to stay.

He took her wrist and pulled her toward the door. "I know it's the wrong time," he said almost against her temple.

"You don't know things about me."

"Like what? You can't imagine what I do know about people."

"Not like me."

"What are you trying to—" And then he stopped. "I forgot something."

"What?" Her heart was banging like a cannon even though she prided herself on the control that had gotten her through rehab and AA without a misstep so far.

"I need to go to the greenhouse."

On an exhale, Daphne laughed, part shock, part amusement, a hundred percent awareness that Patrick was a mystery to her.

"I know," he said, "but you might as well realize I'm tangled up in family. Miriam developed a rose for my mother, and I give her one for Mother's Day every year."

"Okay. I'll get Miriam."

"No, thanks." He tugged at his tie and his tailor-made collar. "I can find her, but you and I are going to talk."

He disappeared through the doorway to the back, and Daphne sagged against the counter. Miriam's voice lifted as she greeted Patrick with gladness. His rumbled in return.

Like a high-school wallflower, Daphne leaned into the hall to get a look at them. Their silhouettes moved toward the greenhouse.

Daphne rubbed her forearms for comfort. She couldn't stand still. She plastered a smile on her face and threw herself into selling flowers and explaining she wasn't Raina.

The store emptied out again while Patrick was with Miriam. Their voices preceded them, coming back.

"I appreciate it," Patrick said.

The clock ticked over the door. Daphne still had deliveries to make. She should leave now, but she couldn't make herself use that door before Patrick did.

How long since she'd felt anything except horror at her bad judgment and fear that she'd drink again? She should be thinking of Raina, worrying about the conversation they had to get through tonight.

Family mattered. A man with priorities of his own did not…could not…matter to her.

"I owe your mother everything," Miriam was saying. "She started me in business, and she showed me what to do with the roses. I enjoyed the time she spent with me here."

"It's a shame her greenhouse is sitting neglected, but you know Mom. She bounces from one interest to the next. Interior design is her newest thing. You'll be lucky if she doesn't drop by with Will in tow to coordinate your color palette."

Miriam laughed. "I'll bolt the door if she shows up."

"What do I owe you?"

"The Gloria is on the house."

"Thanks, but I want to pay," he said. "It's my gift for her."

"You never change, Patrick." She rested her fist against his shoulder. "Daphne will check you out."

Patrick stopped, smiling as he set a long-stemmed rose on the counter. A mauve ribbon matched the bud bursting to bloom.

"Need my card again?" he asked.

"Uh-uh. Thanks." Daphne's fingers refused to obey again. She fumbled with the buttons on the cash register and had to start over.

Daphne finished his transaction and wrapped his rose in pale pink tissue, marked with Miriam's logo, and then she found a box, in which she nestled the rose in more tissue.

Patrick waited by the counter, making her nervous. "Did you manage to talk to Raina?" he asked.

"I'm seeing her after work tonight." She could just imagine his reaction to the stories she had to tell her sister.

"Good. She needs you."

"That was the last thing I expected you to say. Have you talked to her?"

"I know her." He balanced the box in one hand and went toward the door. Daphne followed him. He pushed against the weight of the door with his free hand. "Maybe you need each other."

"Wait." She grabbed his arm. Cool air swept in around his shoulder. More spring showers on the way. "Why are you saying these things? You don't know me."

He shook his head and let his fingertips rest against her cheek. When she leaned against his hand, he bent down. His lips brushed hers. Need met need, sheer physical relief spun into urgency.

Suddenly, it was as if she were a spectator. She saw Patrick, his back to the open door, and herself, lifting her hands to his face because she couldn't stop, and then she imagined Miriam bursting out of the back or one of Patrick's neighbors literally stumbling across them.

She broke away, staring at him, stunned and yet eager for him to take the decision away from her, to take her in his arms again.

"I know you," he said. "And you know me. Isn't it like that sometimes?"

"I KNOW YOU," he'd said while his kiss had still burned on her mouth. But in fact, he didn't. When he really understood the truth about her, how would he feel?

The old Daphne would have fled, the better portion of a fifth of whiskey in her gut, and the rest of the bottle tucked safely close at hand in the glove box. The new Daphne turned the lock on the door at Bundle of Blooms, leaving Miriam to her greenhouse work.

She still had Raina to face.

Daphne walked quickly to her car and climbed in to lean her forehead against the steering wheel.

She pulled Raina's envelope from her purse and committed the chicken-scratch directions to memory. When she dropped the envelope on the seat again, she saw the return address and laughed.

Raina's platinum-credit-card bill. Unopened. The girl might have money, but good Lord, she needed someone to carry around her common sense and remind her to use it. Daphne tucked the bill back into her purse.

Finding her sister's house in the stratified neighborhoods of Honesty proved a little more difficult than Daphne had anticipated. The directions hadn't mentioned twisting roads that changed names and then changed back.

Old money lived in the row houses, like Patrick. She turned away from his street and ended up heading toward the line of Victorian manses on a hill that overlooked the square.

The Abernathy estate clung to that hill among the gingerbread and brick monstrosities that acted as gargoyles repelling bad spirits from the sweet little town.

At last she found the newly resurfaced black road that wound into the neighborhood on the hill.

Raina's place was in the first line of homes. An elegant A like the one on Raina's silverware was scrawled into the wrought-iron gates. Three stories of brick and wavy-paned windows stood behind hedges and graceful trees and bulbs coming to color in the form of lilies and crocuses and blood-red tulips.

The gates stayed closed.

An intercom speaker was embedded in a brick stanchion close to the driver's side of the car. Daphne opened her window and punched the button to speak. "Raina?"

Static answered her. She listened hard for a voice, but static rattled again into the otherwise still night.

The gate swung open.

"Thanks," Daphne said, rolling her eyes for a glimpse of spruce branches and darkening sky. "I'll be right up. Don't loose the hounds upon me."

"You like to make fun, don't you?"

"Raina, you can speak. I thought you were sending Morse code in static bursts. I'll be there before you know it."

The driveway wound like a snake through formal plantings, cut back for winter but beginning to bud. Not a dot of anything untoward touched the velvet lawn. The Abernathys must have spent more than Daphne's best annual salary on landscaping and maintenance.

Her sister opened the big glossy black door and came onto her wide porch like Scarlett welcoming the Tarletons.

Daphne parked and jumped out of the car. "I expected the old family retainer."

"Who would that be?"

Raina's spike-edged tone deflated Daphne's flippancy. "I guess that would be Patrick," she said, feeling more vulnerable just from saying his name. "You aren't hiding him in there somewhere?"

"Come search if you'd like."

"I forgot my posse."

"Your—"

"My hotel TV barely picks up *Gunsmoke* reruns on some local channel. I'm becoming an expert on the American western." She stayed on the first brick step. "I've never seen a place like this that wasn't a museum. Or a castle. I'm not sure I belong."

"Come inside and stop making a big deal about it. We shut the dungeon down generations ago. Keeping the rack in good repair really saps the capital."

Daphne followed her twin up the steps and inside

the cool, wide hall. Victorian darkness shrouded the place in shadows.

"You need more windows."

"You don't have to be nervous. Tell me what happened to you."

What had she expected? A chair as comfortable as any rack and an invitation to tea?

"Can we start with your college thing? I'm sorry about hurting your feelings. I put you on a pedestal and I didn't expect you to be human." She held up her hands, begging for a truce. "I like you human. I prefer you human because there's some chance you'll be able to deal with the rest of what I have to tell you."

"That was my only big secret, and I wasn't eager to share it, but I thought it would be safe with you." Raina went to a spot on the wall and light flooded the hall. Sort of flooded. Heavy, scrolled furniture drew more sinister shadows that seemed to hover. "Telling you took nerve," Raina said.

Daphne nodded. "I let you down, but I didn't mean to. You surprised me. I hardly know you, but I already assume you won't choose to do something wrong."

Raina rubbed her face. "I made a bad choice in college, and I get ashamed when I think about it, But I'm also sorry I stomped out like a teenager, and if it matters, I only did a few papers. I couldn't take the guilt back then, either."

Without thinking, Daphne hugged her sister. "You don't have to explain anything to me."

Raina hugged back. "I didn't expect you to get upset."

"Yeah?"

"Don't assume I mean because you're an arch-criminal or something. I just thought that because you'd lived more, you'd understand more."

Daphne's heart melted for the second time that day. "I'm so sorry I didn't."

"Let's call a truce." With her arms still around her sister, Raina eased Daphne toward the kitchen. "Come to the kitchen. I'll make us sandwiches."

"We'll make them together. You'll need plenty of sustenance before the night is over." Daphne stopped before an actual suit of armor. "Don't you have a horde of servants to wait on you and throw that thing into the dungeon?"

"You really have funny ideas. My trust fund pays a limited amount, and I have bills. I can barely afford Mrs. Dodge, the woman who makes sure I eat daily, but my mother would rise like an avenging angel if I tried to let her go. She usually leaves something, but I told her I wasn't hungry because I thought we'd have sandwiches."

"I like the privacy."

"You can escape without anyone knowing you were here?"

They reached a long kitchen bound by tall windows, paned with wavy glass. "Don't kid yourself, Raina. You may want me to disappear like a bad dream."

"Sure I will." Raina went to a porcelain sink as big as any bathtub Daphne had ever seen. She turned off the evening news on a TV that looked out of place in an alcove set among period cabinets above a lime- stone counter.

"This room is bigger than most apartments I've lived in," Daphne said. "And you have all the comforts. The TV's kind of small for a rich girl, but—good grief—it's high definition."

"You're nervous again."

"I'm going to be until we've had our talk."

Raina washed her hands. "You act like you won't be my sister if I don't approve, but look at us. We're together for life even if we both decide we loathe each other."

Raina dried her hands and hung the towel on a rail. Then she wrapped her arms around her waist, a gesture that also came naturally to Daphne. She would have bet her next breath that her sister didn't know she looked afraid.

"I didn't lead your kind of life," Daphne said.

Raina's folded arms slipped a little. She tossed Daphne a look that said "Duh" loud and clear.

"I had some bad luck with foster families." In her head, a memory began to take form—a door squeak- ing open to let in a thin strand of light. She pushed it away, breathing hard. "So I ran away. A couple of times."

"What happened to you?"

Nope. Raina wasn't ready to hear that yet, and Daphne wasn't ready to tell. "I was a kid when I ran away. I couldn't exactly find a job, and I stole some things. Food, mostly. Once, a book."

"Why didn't you go to the police?"

It was her turn to flash the "Duh" look. "Where would they send me? Another foster home—or back to the same one. I wasn't adoptable."

"Who would have been, after a childhood like that?" Raina started toward her.

Daphne wanted to walk into her sister's arms, but she held out both hands. "You'd better hear the rest. I tried a—substance or two."

"Daphne, I want to know exactly what you did. Don't soften the facts for me."

"I try too hard when I'm nervous. Remember?"

"Don't, with me."

"I don't feel entirely safe yet. Let me finish. I got a clue after I was sent back to the one house where I'd felt sort of safe."

"They took care of you?"

"It's never that simple, Raina. I was too busy protecting myself to let anyone take care of me, and I just wanted out, but a friend of mine was there, too, and we promised to look out for each other."

"But?"

She hesitated, but forced herself to go on, in a rush. "My friend overdosed. She was pregnant and scared and she didn't want to think about it so she died, and I got totally clean and stayed in school and actually did the work. Afterward, I managed to persuade the D.A. and a judge to seal my juvenile record so I'd have a chance with the colleges I wanted."

"How'd you pay for school?"

"Not with scholarships, for sure. I pushed grocery

carts anytime I could get a shift at the local market, and I read SAT exam guides in libraries until I could pass with an acceptable score." She caught her breath, lifting her face to find her twin's imprinted with dread.

"When did you start going to AA?" Raina asked.

Daphne shook her head, so lost in getting all the truth out, she barely understood. "I got a degree in criminology on the fast track, and I found a job as a jury consultant. One good thing about my kind of life, I knew people. I had to be able to size up a guy or I could end up…" Again, she'd let herself slip out of bounds. "Hurt," she said. "And people begged me to work for them, almost from my first case. I read truth the way most people read their own names. I mean, I could tell who was lying right away. I could tell which potential juror the lawyers should select to make the case go our client's way."

"That's good."

"Until Milton Stegwell."

"Milton—"

She lifted her hands, this time pleading. It was almost over. "Good God, the pictures in my head," she said, and Raina flinched. "Crime-scene photos. They'll follow me until the day I fall into my own grave."

"Stop, Daphne."

"In a second."

"I can't move."

"I don't mean to frighten you, but you have to know everything because this is who I am."

"You're not some guy who obviously did something unforgivable."

"He killed his wife and their three children, but back then I believed he was innocent. I only chose juries for innocent defendants. Until he bragged about destroying his family after his acquittal, I would have bet every stick of furniture in my safe and tasteful apartment. I would have handed over the keys to my Jag to pay for his defense. I almost did his case for free because he was so damn misunderstood."

"God."

"Yeah. I've done some praying since that case. Nothing scares you more than the innocent blood of three children and their real live loving mother. She fought for her children. She gave her life for them. She loved them, and he killed her and their babies, and I helped him go free."

Her legs wobbled. She grabbed the cool limestone counter.

"Daphne." Raina reached for her. "He's the one who should feel this guilt."

"I was part of his defense. I can't shut my eyes and say it was just a job. I helped recommend the people who set him free." They held on to each other. Daphne couldn't stop. "He sent us a note afterward—something about how you really can broadcast your guilt on the evening news if a jury thinks you're innocent."

"Let me talk for a second." Raina, weak and sheltered and rabbit-like in Patrick's office, was stronger than Daphne now. "You did nothing wrong. That man had to be psychotic. How could you expect to see through him?"

Daphne staggered out of her sister's arms, slipping against the counter. "Because I've been a bad person, too. I know how to lie. I know what to look for, but he fooled me. He could marry another innocent woman and then kill her and her children, too."

"No, he can't. You and I will find him and make sure wherever he goes, people know what he did."

Daphne smiled, despite the fact that Milton and his crimes had all but destroyed her life. "You're vengeful."

"When it comes to family."

"The D.A. had the same plan. He asked for volunteers in his office to keep tabs on Milton."

"You can't do more. I'm not naive," Raina said. "You did your job and this creep fooled you. I'm surprised his attorney didn't resign."

"We visited a bar or two together, wallowing in guilt. That's why I try not to think about it. Guilt is a good excuse to drink."

"Not ever again."

Daphne had saved the worst for last, and shame nearly choked her. "I hope you're right. I plan never to drink again because I got a DUI after I took out a power pole about eight months ago. Once they stitched up my head—" she showed the scar above her ear "—I had a night in jail to think what might have happened after I got behind the wheel of that car." Daphne pressed her fists into her eyes and then tried to laugh. "I must seem even more of a hypocrite being shocked that you'd written a couple of assignments for pay."

"Forget it."

Daphne stared at her. "It's that easy for you to forgive me?"

Raina came to her again and refused to let her move away when she held her. "You're so tough. What you need is to forgive yourself."

It was good to lean against Raina. Her sister. Her family.

"I want you to like me. I'm scared you won't."

"Maybe I feel the same about you."

It was strange, exactly what she'd hoped for, and yet, silence pressed against her ears. As a finale for tonight's performance, she might just faint.

"Why did you tell me all of this now?" Raina asked.

"For the same reason I had my last whiskey about half an hour before I hit that pole. I work best with pristine starts, and I didn't want you to stumble across something that might make you think I'd kept the truth from you—or even tried to shade it."

Daphne saw a mother's patience in Raina's eyes. Maybe only a woman who'd been raised by a good mother could be so kind and so strong.

"I am human. I understand choices, and you are my family now. We're going to say things that hurt each other."

Daphne smiled. "You amaze me."

"Because you don't expect enough for yourself. Open your eyes. You don't need to be punished. You've been trying to do that killer's penance. You don't think you deserve a good life."

Raina turned to a white tin with a loaf of bread

painted on its front. Daphne grabbed the counter again and finally gasped as if she'd fallen from a great height, landed on her back and…survived.

CHAPTER SEVEN

RAINA TURNED, drawn to the rasp of Daphne's breathing. "What's the matter with you?"

"I guess we're going to say things that heal, too." She yanked a stool away from the counter and collapsed onto it.

"What did I say?"

"I've been trying to do that man's time."

Raina opened the bread box. "The trick is to see yourself without guilt. You aren't like him. You think you're a bad person, but you've spent your entire adult life making sure you aren't."

"So the trick is to believe I don't need to do penance."

"It's not a trick," Raina said. "You simply have to see yourself the way I see you."

"Maybe I can't do it that way. Thinking I'm not bad takes some practice after all these years."

"You had lousy foster care. I wonder why my parents didn't adopt us both."

"I guess we'll never find out, but maybe they didn't know about me," Daphne said.

"I hate what your life has done to you."

Daphne hated the amount of time she'd wasted assuming she'd be wrong for everyone. Even this afternoon, when Patrick had kissed her, she'd pulled away, thinking she was the kind of woman who'd be a bigger problem for him after his ugly divorce.

"Raina, can I ask you a question I have no right to ask?"

"Maybe." She took out four slices of bread. Still holding it in one hand, she managed to open a cupboard and pull down plates.

"Are you in love with Patrick?"

The plates clattered to the counter. "What is the matter with people in this town? Who told you that?"

"You did, with the way you depend on him."

Raina stared at her for a second before she set the bread on the plates. "You've read me wrong. He's my friend, nothing more. What makes you ask?"

"I don't want to be his friend," Daphne said.

Raina paused at the fridge. "Meaning?"

"I've only known him for a couple of weeks." Daphne crossed to a mesh basket beside the stove and chose a tomato from a rich, red pile of them. "But I care about him." She pretended the tomato fascinated her. "I think. I'd like to find out, if you won't be hurt."

The fridge door opened. From the sound of things, Raina was searching for something specific. At last a glass jar connected with the counter.

Daphne turned to see if Raina needed help, but no, she'd set fancy mustard on the limestone.

"I don't mind if you see Patrick," she said.

"It may come to nothing. I don't want him to come between us."

"Does he feel the way you do?"

"I'm not sure." She didn't know how to answer. She couldn't talk about the kiss.

"His ex-wife is addicted to prescription drugs. He's going to be afraid when you tell him about your problem," Raina said. "I don't want you to hurt each other."

THAT NIGHT, when she left Raina's, she dialed Patrick's number. He answered just after the first ring.

"Daphne?"

"About that talk."

"Where are you?"

"In my car. I'd like to meet you somewhere, but I know you have your son."

"I can't get a sitter this late. Maybe we could meet tomorrow night."

"Can I come to your house?" Daphne said. She'd rather tell him about her alcoholism before gossip got to him first.

"Don't take this the wrong way," he said, "but I wouldn't want my son to see you here, and he might wake up."

"I'm not suggesting a sleepover," she said.

"I don't want to confuse him."

Raina had said he was overprotective. "Maybe you could come outside to talk to me."

"I was thinking dinner, or at least comfortable chairs," he said.

"I'm not sure we'll need that."

"I'm damn near seduced already. Come on over. You can have Will's tire swing and I'll sit on our oak tree's roots."

"I don't have your address."

"I'll talk you here. Where are you now?"

"I'm getting close to the square. Going up to Raina's seemed to take longer than coming down."

"Have you been thinking about this afternoon?"

The kiss. "I guess I haven't thought of much else. That's why I need to tell you some things."

"I'm not sure what you mean."

She didn't blame a single father whose ex-wife had nearly neglected their son to death for putting up his guard. "I'll tell you in a few minutes."

"I remember the curve of your waist," he said. "I can still feel it against my palms. Wanting you is so intense I feel as if I've recognized you even though we don't know each other very well. I never believed I'd feel this way."

She concentrated on breathing and avoiding the poles along the road. "I'm almost at the square."

"Take the first red light after the square. Turn left. I like the way you taste, too, Daphne."

"Please don't say that."

"I like the way your voice goes husky when you look at me."

"How many times has that happened?"

"The other day, when I saw you on the bench. Today, when I kissed you. You know I want more from you. I want to touch all of you. Now."

"I'm turning left."

"You should be on Bryerly. I'm in the yard."

He walked into the pooled illumination of a street-light. Daphne parked at the first open spot on the street. Her heart raced as she walked toward him. He came out of the streetlight. There was no mistaking the desire in his eyes.

He caught her close. She ducked away from his mouth, but his lips trailed across her cheek. He kissed the pulse beneath her jawline.

"People might be watching," she said.

"Come through here."

A wooden gate opened in the brick wall that surrounded his house. A brief walkway took them to the back, where a rope swing shone in the moonlight and an oak's thick trunk stood guard over the otherwise empty lawn.

"I wasn't kidding," he said. "There's no place to sit."

"Over there." She pointed to the steps on a brick patio just outside his backdoor.

"They'll be chilly now that it's dark."

She sat but found she didn't know how to start her second confession of the day.

"What do you want to tell me?" Patrick asked.

"About my past."

"Is it any of my business?"

"Don't get scared. I'm not suggesting a lifetime commitment, but Raina told me about your ex-wife."

"I wish she hadn't."

"You'll understand if you let me finish." But the

lighted windows above her presented a moment of justified procrastination. "What if Will wakes up?"

Patrick pulled a monitor from his jacket pocket. "I'll hear him."

"He can't hear us?" The last thing that little boy needed was the story of another woman who couldn't resist the allure of oblivion.

"No." Patrick speared his fingers through her hair. "What can you have to tell me? You know I looked you up. I found your record in track and a news story about a bike accident when you broke your wrist."

"I never broke my wrist." Normally, she'd have objected to anyone snooping, but she understood that Patrick was being cautious.

"I found the wrong Daphne Soder?"

She nodded and he sat beside her, stretching his legs in front of him. She looked up, drawn to the glitter in his eyes. As cool air swirled between them, she felt more detached from him than she had since he'd touched her arm in his office lobby

"You found a nice innocuous girl with my name, but I'm not like her."

He stared at his feet. Somewhere, a horn honked. Her heart tight with regret, Daphne wished she was sitting in this same spot, next to Patrick, hearing about his day, telling him about the things she'd done. Nice things that hadn't hurt anyone.

He lifted his head, "What did you do, Daphne?"

"Telling you seems premature and extreme. We don't know each other well, but Raina and I talked tonight and something she said convinced me to tell you."

"I don't need to be massaged. Just give me the truth."

"It started—I don't remember when…" She spoke slowly. Life drained from his expression with each word. He didn't interrupt, but he didn't have to. He never moved a muscle, but she felt him pulling away all the same. She finally finished with the meeting at the church.

"After I talked to Raina, I wanted to tell you before someone who saw me there mentioned it."

He nodded, his mouth a thin line.

"You knew I couldn't afford to bring another addict into my son's life."

"I guessed you might feel that way. I'm not an addict," she said. "But the feelings between us are strong, and I didn't want you to confuse me for someone safe like Raina, for instance."

"You know that my son nearly died because I was blind to my wife's problems."

"That's why I came tonight. To tell you about mine." She stood. "I need to move. I already know what you're going to decide."

"He's my son, Daphne, just a baby, and he can't decide whether being with you might be worth the risk. Hell, I can't decide that, even though I've never wanted a woman the way I want you." He stood, as well, and pulled her into his arms. He was warmth in a world that felt ice-coated, and he was life on a night when she'd finally begun to believe she had a right to live. He turned her in his arms, and her legs slid between his. Their thighs met and she wouldn't have said no if he'd lowered her to the ground. She couldn't speak for wanting him. "But I can't believe these feelings last because they seem so overwhelming."

"Then why are you doing this?" she asked, her voice hoarse. He was also aroused. He'd left her in no doubt. "You're saying goodbye, but your body…"

"Wants a woman it cannot have."

She turned toward the glow of the streetlight on his brick wall. "I have to go."

"What did you think I would say?" He grabbed the rope swing as if he wanted to pull her back but didn't dare. "I want to pretend it doesn't matter and I'll trust that you won't drink."

"But I'm damaged goods?" She pushed his hand away. "There was a time when I would have agreed. Hell, maybe that was this morning, but I've been working since the day I was arrested on trying to do the right thing. I may be damaged, but I haven't touched a drop since I climbed out of that car. I work hard at staying sober."

"And what about the day something makes you feel bad enough to drink again? Something that acts like whatever triggered you before?"

"I can't think that way." Raina and her talk of penance put some steel in Daphne's backbone. "The things that triggered my thirst were guilt and living without love. Raina said tonight that I was trying to do Milton Stegwell's time. Well, I've done more than he ever will, and I finally believe I'm worthy of love.

I might make mistakes again, but one of them won't be choosing a man who believes the worst about me."

"I don't."

"I know." She stopped at his gate. "You just have to prepare yourself for the chance that it might happen. I understand it's because of Will. I don't even blame you. But that fear of yours makes you the wrong man for me. I need trust and you can't give that."

She'd made her stand, grabbed at a future she deserved. All her life she'd assumed that kind of future was closed off to the little orphan who'd never been loved. Tonight, that girl had begun to heal herself after a long battle.

And, as she slammed the gate, she tried to convince herself that Patrick was a fool for losing his chance with her. Still, deep inside, she suspected she might have done the same thing if Will were her child.

WILL SWUNG from Patrick's hand as they walked Gloria out to the car on Mother's Day morning. "Ooh, Grandma, can we get a hamburger for lunch?"

"Sure. We'll go to Draper's Diner," she said.

Edna Draper had been Patrick's babysitter when he was Will's age. She'd opened the diner after her husband's untimely death had forced her to make up for the deficit in his company's pension plan. Mrs. Draper's food was good, the ingredients hand-chosen, organic and healthy.

"See, Dad? I told you Grandma wouldn't mind."

"Are you sure you don't want something fancier?" Patrick asked.

"Edna needs her friends to drop in today. She opens because none of her children live in town anymore."

Patrick helped Will fasten his seat belt and then checked the booster seat to make sure it was secure. "Today is Raina's first Mother's Day alone."

His mother immediately rummaged in her purse and pulled out a fancy cell phone that made Patrick's look like something out of Alexander Graham Bell's lab. She punched in a single number and waited.

Nothing appeared to happen.

"She's not answering," Gloria said.

"Should we go by the house?"

His mother paused to consider. Then she flipped the phone shut. "She's a big girl. She may have made other plans, and she doesn't need us nursemaiding her the way her parents did."

They could call Daphne. The thought passed through his mind, but he discarded it with an eye on his son in the rearview mirror.

"Can I play your phone game, Grandma?" Will strained to reach it, sticking out his feet. He was getting so tall his toes brushed the back of Patrick's seat. He wouldn't need the booster much longer. "Fix it for me."

She set up the game and passed her phone back to him. "Things are looking better around here," she said.

Will hit the buttons without a care about anything except winning. Patrick had to believe he'd made the right decision. The status quo was the best environment for his son.

But then he remembered Daphne in his arms, her

hands clinging to his shoulders, her slender hips cradling him until she'd pulled abruptly away.

The wheels were coming off that bus he and Will often sang about. He glanced at his mother, trying not to see Daphne last night, proud and furious, walking out of his life.

"You sure about the hamburger?" She'd recently become vegetarian except for the meals she cooked for him and Will.

"I talked to Edna about her menu. She's put in a wonderful stir-fry for me."

"You have pull."

"I like that smile on you."

"Feels kind of funny." He rubbed his chin, hating that his mother had noticed the change in him since the final episode with Lisa. "Will could use a dad who smiles."

"Will bounces back." His mother folded her hands on her lap. "You're doing a good job with him, but I worry about you."

"Mom," he said, glancing pointedly into the rearview.

His mother nodded. "I'll keep quiet for now, but something's made you more edgy than usual this morning. A mother knows."

Startled by her directness, he laughed. "Where is the reserved woman who raised me without addressing a problem head-on?"

"She got wiser. The world is different, and there's one subject I wish I had addressed with you, over and over."

After the divorce he'd discovered she'd never been sure of Lisa. "I'm fine," he said, and he did feel better. He'd chosen wrong again, even letting himself begin to fall for Daphne, but at least he knew that he was capable of caring. That gave him hope.

"As I said, we'll talk later." She pointed through the windshield. "Look at the crowd today."

Draper's parking had spilled into Emily's Doll Hospital's lot next door. Emily had closed for Mother's Day. Patrick got out and went to help Will, but the back door opened and his son jumped onto the pavement, still involved with his game.

"When did you learn to undo the seatbelt?"

"Dad," Will said in the same don't-bug-me tone Patrick had used to ease his mother out of his private thoughts.

"Why don't you put that away for now?" Patrick touched his mother's phone.

Gloria stopped at the corner of Emily's store. "He can hold on to it. Look at this line."

It wound out of the restaurant's doorway and stopped at Emily's row of comfy rockers. Patrick's stomach growled. He and Will laughed. "You didn't slip any of your homemade bread into your purse, did you, Mother?"

"My word."

Her answer indicated that she wasn't paying attention. Then he saw the two women who'd provoked it. Raina and Daphne, looking identical except for their clothing. Daphne wore jeans and a pale peach T-shirt that glowed against her skin and hugged her breasts before it flared to her hips. Raina had on the usual suit, this time in lime green.

They stood, smiling at each other, shyly, like new friends feeling their way. Resenting his illogical annoyance that Raina—not he—was with Daphne, he maneuvered Will in front of him, resting his hands on his boy's shoulders. The morning breeze pushed Daphne's T-shirt against her, outlining her body with loving, invisible fingers.

"Mom, did I tell you Miriam wants her store redecorated?"

"Does she?"

She sounded so excited he felt guilty. "Sorry, bad joke." Unsettled, remembering the thrust of Daphne's sweet, round breasts against his chest, he'd searched for something to say. "I told her you were apprenticing on my house and she said she'd bar her doors if she saw you coming."

"She's smarter than that. I'll drop by and show her what I can do."

"I was kidding."

"It's a good idea, though, and it takes my mind off wanting to grill you about those young girls."

"Women," he said, looking away from the glint of a gold medal in the dark vee between Daphne's breasts. He'd never had the chance to kiss her there. He never would.

She turned her head slightly. Her eyes widened, and then a smile touched her mouth. A slight smile that undid his determination.

He felt himself smile back, breathing around an

ache that squeezed his chest. He'd done everything the right way with Lisa. Would finding a different way with Daphne be so wrong? If Will never knew her, he couldn't be hurt.

Patrick wiped moist palms down the legs of his jeans. What if he hurt Daphne because he was so desperate to be with her?

CHAPTER EIGHT

DAPHNE TRIED not to bring up the subject of Patrick while she and Raina shared their meal. And she was successful until a lull in conversation made her speak.

"His son looks healthy." Daphne turned quickly to look without getting caught. The little boy was still playing a game on a cell phone. His blond hair looked almost white against Patrick's dark blue shirt. He was leaning against his father, and they both seemed intent on the phone's keyboard.

But Daphne had a feeling Patrick was aware of her, too.

"Why did you smile at him?" Raina asked. "You shouldn't let him off the hook. He's my best friend, and *I'd* like to take a swing at him."

Daphne stopped in midbite. "That's exactly what I don't want," she said. Spinach salad dropped off her fork. "Coming between you two would make me feel worse than having to face him all over again."

"He's a defense attorney. He's seen a lot and he knows people can change. I'm disappointed in him."

"But this could affect his child." Daphne shrugged.

"He can't help the way he feels, and I understand why he's wary. I thought you would be, too."

"You're too good to be true."

"I have a talent for knowing the way people think. You're not concerned that the people who know you in this town—and that would be everyone—will look at you differently because of me?"

"I don't want to care." She said it so low Daphne had to lean forward. "Explain to me." Raina sipped her soup from her spoon in perfect, delicate silence. "You told me the truth. You care about Patrick and you faced him with all your worst secrets, even though you knew your relationship—"

"It was too new for that." And she'd destroyed it.

"How do you manage to stop caring what people think of you?"

"So you do care, Raina?"

"Sure. My parents wanted certain things for me, and I don't want to let their memory down."

"What if I make things difficult for you? You have to know some people will look down their noses at me, especially when someone else sees me going down those stairs at the church. Did you just pretend it wouldn't matter?"

Raina shook her head. "You moved here with the stuff in your car and the clothes on your back, and you were willing to leave when I didn't greet you with open arms. You've done everything for yourself, without the help of parents or friends. Even the system that should have protected you put you in danger. You have courage."

"I understand fear. I didn't want to be in more danger, so I avoided it. Even when I came here, I planned to depart if you didn't want a twin. But you marched straight across your kitchen when I needed you most, and you put your arms around a perfect stranger who happened to be your sister."

"I guess if we take turns being strong, we'll make a good team." Raina speared some field greens with an innocent smile on her face. "And Patrick? Did you tell him he already mattered to you?"

"That's exactly the kind of risk you'd take, but I couldn't. I gave him the facts, and they were too much for him."

"Notice I'm not offering to talk to him for you." Raina's eyes warmed with a mixture of empathy and affection over her tea glass. "I know you want him to decide, even though I could assure him I believe in you."

To Daphne's surprise, Raina's loyalty brought the sting of tears. "You don't have any more reason to believe in me than he does."

"But I won't change." Looking over Daphne's shoulder, Raina got serious. "His mother's coming over."

Daphne froze. She feared she might bend her fork.

"Excuse me." His mother had a slightly less blue version of his icy eyes, but hers were kinder. "Raina, how are you today?"

"Happy Mother's Day, Gloria." Raina stood and only allowed the shadow of grief to touch her face as she hugged the older woman. "I'm all right." She held her hand out toward Daphne. "Have you met my sister?"

"Obviously, you're Daphne." Gloria touched Daphne's shoulder, staring. "I'm pleased to meet you."

"Hello." Daphne stood, as well. She felt Patrick's presence as if he were part of the conversation.

"I won't keep you, but I thought this day might be a bit difficult for you, Raina. Call if you want to talk, and Daphne, you drop by with Raina."

"Thanks." Raina hugged her friend again. "You're thoughtful to come over."

"Nonsense." But her smile held motherly affection. "I'll hope to run into you both again soon." Mrs. Gannon looked at her table where Will had gone back to a toy and Patrick was looking cold and intense again.

From across the room, his message was clear: Stay away from me and mine.

Gloria walked away, but not without curiosity.

"Raina, I don't mean to gossip, but you said Patick's ex neglected Will. What exactly did she do?"

"She left him in her car one day last winter while she went into a shop, and then she overdosed in the dressing room."

"Where is she now?"

"I don't know. She left town after the judge told her she couldn't see Will until she cleaned up."

Daphne looked down at her plate. "And Patrick's afraid I'm like her?"

"She refuses to admit she has a problem, Daphne. You're taking care of yours."

"I wonder if Patrick could ever believe that."

"He looks at you as if he wants to." Raina stabbed at the lettuce on her plate again.

Daphne turned her head. Gloria and Will had their heads bent over something they were writing together. Patrick's gaze, hot and hungry, crossed the room and ignited the feelings she was trying to keep under control.

She wanted to be angry, but her body went heavy with need. Her pulse ricocheted as she felt the simple thrill of hope. She wasn't like his ex-wife, and surely he was intelligent enough to see that.

As if he were reading her mind, he shook his head, just enough for her to see. Then he cradled his son's head in the palm of his hand. Will turned toward him with a sweet, guileless grin.

"Everything you feel shows on your face," Raina said. "If Patrick could really see you, he'd know you'd never hurt Will."

"I see a man who loves his son." Her voice felt thick as she remembered the pressure of his legs against hers. He'd danced her across his yard, almost to the gate. "He could love a woman that much, too."

PATRICK SPENT A WEEK of sleepless nights. Every time he closed his eyes, he felt the vibration of Daphne's pulse against his lips. He dreamed of peeling that peach-colored shirt off her. Then he dreamed of tearing it off. As he ran his hands from her waist to the curves of her breasts, frustration woke him.

Night after night.

He wasn't sleeping. He wasn't paying close enough attention to his work. He'd been late to court this morning, and now he was running back to his office for a file he should have had with him.

He'd felt as if he'd had no choice when he'd let Daphne walk away, but wanting her in his sleep wasn't making things easier.

His cell phone rang as he rushed into the elevator. He flipped the top open.

"Patrick, it's Mother. I'm picking Will up at school today."

"What's wrong?" He pushed his hand between the closing elevator doors and forced them open again so he could get out. "Is he sick?"

"I had a strange call from Lisa and I wonder if she might not be in town. She asked me where Will is."

"What?" His bark turned the heads of every human in the lobby. He ducked into one of the alcoves. "Did she say she's in town? Call the cops, Mom. He didn't shut his eyes for two weeks the last time she tried to grab him."

"Maybe I'll take him out of school early."

"I shouldn't have sent that flower arrangement to Lisa for him."

"Your son wanted his mother to have a gift. You had no choice. I'm leaving now to pick him up."

"And bring him to my office."

"No, no. You have to work, and we don't want to alarm Will." She tapped something against the receiver. "I'll take him to the park by the courthouse.

We'll have a picnic. He can swing and climb on the fort and run till he's too tired to breathe. And you can look out and see him whenever you need to."

He'd rather have him in his office or in the courtroom. "He might get bored after a few hours."

"Not with my trusty cell phone. Video games are a grandma's best friend. In my day, Grandma's best friend was her dress-up trunk, but I don't really see Will in Victorian cuffs and collars."

"Thanks, Mother."

"Think nothing of it. I'm on my way to his school. You might put in a call to warn them I'll be checking him out."

"I'll do it right now."

"And I'll call when I have him."

"Okay, but I'll be in court for a few more hours this afternoon. We have the plea bargain in place, but Hal has to allocute."

"If you don't answer, I'll leave a message."

My son. "If only I'd been smarter with Lisa. I wanted to believe her lies about the drugs and the phony illnesses."

"You aren't responsible for Lisa's crimes." She took a deep breath. "I'm not saying anything more."

"I'll see you in a while." He started to close his phone but brought it back to his ear. "Mother, if you need me, and I don't answer, call back right away. I'll leave the phone on vibrate in my pocket, and I'll explain in court if I have to. What's a little contempt?"

"Sounds good. Try not to panic. Your son will be fine."

FREE BOOKS OFFER

To get you started, we'll send you
2 FREE books and a FREE gift

There's no catch, everything is **FREE**

Accepting your 2 **FREE** books and **FREE** mystery gift
places you under no obligation to buy anything.

Be part of the Mills & Boon® Book Club™ and receive your favourite
Series books up to 2 months before they are in the shops and delivered
straight to your door. Plus, enjoy a wide range of **EXCLUSIVE** benefits!

- Best new women's fiction – delivered right to
  your door with FREE P&P

- Avoid disappointment – get your books up to
  2 months before they are in the shops

- No contract – no obligation to buy

We hope that after receiving your free books you'll
want to remain a member. But the choice is yours.
So why not give us a go? You'll be glad you did!

Visit **millsandboon.co.uk** to stay up to date
with offers and to sign-up for our newsletter

2 **FREE** books
and a
FREE gift

S0CIA

Mrs/Miss/Ms/Mr _____ Initials _____

BLOCK CAPITALS PLEASE

Surname _____

Address _____

Postcode _____

Email _____

MILLS & BOON®

MILLS & BOON®
Book Club

FREE BOOK OFFER
FREEPOST NAT 10298
RICHMOND
TW9 1BR

NO STAMP
NECESSARY
IF POSTED IN
THE U.K. OR N.I.

He went upstairs and grabbed the file from his office. Back in the courthouse conference room they'd been assigned, Alexis was handling the prep for Hal's allocution. Hal found a male too challenging in any situation, so Patrick took care of the paperwork, perched against the window. By the time his mother called to let him know she had Will, he'd already seen them.

She hung up her phone, and they both waved from the playground. He waved back and silently blessed his mother for going beyond the call of duty.

She'd stop Lisa if she had to use a tank, and he'd go through that damn window before he'd give his ex-wife access to their innocent child again.

Patrick turned his laptop so that he only had to look over the top of the screen to see his son and mother working their way along the rope netting. Thank God she'd taken up some sort of commando training.

He settled into his paperwork. This was better. Like shoving half the courthouse off his chest.

IN THE MIDDLE of loading plants into her car for delivery, Daphne lifted her face to the spring sky. Everything seemed to be blooming. And the sound of the laughter from children in the playground inside the courthouse square added to her sense of well-being.

When laughter turned into a scream, Daphne shuddered as if a memory were forming and exploding out of her soul. But this scream was no memory. She straightened, a heavy crystal vase in her hands.

"Grandma, help me, help!"

Men and women dotted the square and the sidewalk. All stopped, all turned like spectators at a sports arena. A man came, half weaving, half running across the lush grass, clutching a little boy beneath his arm like a football.

Will? That guy had Patrick's son.

"Will." Daphne started across the street, vaguely hearing a car's brakes squealing.

"Grandma," the boy keened, wriggling, waving his arms at his grandmother, who ran behind them, terror on her face.

Daphne's heart pounded. The man hadn't seen her. He didn't yet understand that no one was going to hurt Patrick's child in front of her. Ever.

Will's name swelled in her chest, but she gritted her teeth to keep from saying it again and alerting his captor. She suddenly remembered the vase she was still clutching in her hands, slopping water.

Perfect.

Daphne got in front of the man and Will. The man's eyes were all pupil, barely focused. He was obviously high. He looked at her like a rat searching for a way out of a cage.

She knew that look. She'd lived on the streets where that look made a person a mark, a victim. She'd protected too many people on the street when they couldn't save themselves because they were damn near unconscious.

And damn her own soul to hell, she suffered a pang of pity.

The man garbled, not a word, hardly a sound. His hair hung in strands clotted with oil. He lifted his free hand. An open switchblade glinted.

"Oh, for God's sake." She hoisted the vase as high as she could. "Don't make me," she said, knowing too well he wasn't going to listen. Unable to stop hating violence even now and reluctant to chance hurting Will, she knew she had to stop the man.

The vase literally jerked out of her hands.

"Don't dither, girl." Gloria Gannon swung the thick glass into the attacker's head. The vase made a thunking sound and then shattered on the ground and the man wobbled.

Too stoned to actually sense pain, he looked as if he might manage to stand and stay conscious.

But then his body began to react.

Daphne grabbed Will as his captor's legs buckled beneath him. A sense of relief nearly dropped her to her knees. Patrick's child, the boy who meant more to him than anyone or anything, was safe.

Despite Patrick's love, this child had already survived a childhood surprisingly like her own. She cradled him, feeling his pulse pounding all through his body.

"Grandma." He was still clawing his way to her through midair. "Grandma."

Gloria stepped over the man and the glass and took Will from Daphne's arms.

"Go into the courthouse," Daphne said. "I'll call the cops."

"Thanks." Gloria peered at the citizens of Honesty

grouped around them, most with phones out and open, also dialing. "People will talk. After you get through to the police, please call my son. Do you know his number?"

"I'll get in touch with him. He's at work?"

"He may actually be in the courthouse by now."

"I'll find him." Nausea and adrenaline danced inside her.

She gave the necessary details to the 911 dispatcher. All around her, urgent voices spoke. She kept an eye on the unconscious man, lying in eucalyptus and long-stemmed blossoms and the shards of about a month's worth of her salary.

She hung up and called information, asking for Patrick's office number. A detached female voice listed the partners' names. Daphne asked to be connected to Patrick's office.

"Mr. Gannon is not available now. May I give you his assistant?"

"Someone just tried to grab his son on the courthouse square. His mother has Will, and she's taken him inside the courthouse. Can you get word to Patrick?"

"Absolutely. May I tell him who's calling?"

Too frustrated with the woman's slow pace to argue, Daphne gave her name and hung up. Already, two police cars were circling the square, lights strobing, sirens bleating.

They skidded toward the sidewalk and four officers jumped out. The female reached Daphne first. No one else had come any closer to her or the lunatic at her feet.

"Your name, ma'am?"

"Daphne Soder. This man tried to kidnap Will Gannon."

"You stopped him?"

"Not really." She'd hesitated. "The boy's grandmother hit this guy with a vase I was holding."

"Where is Mrs. Gannon?"

No hesitation. She obviously knew Patrick and his mother. "In the courthouse. She took Will to safety, but I think she knows you'll want to speak to her."

"Why don't you tell me what happened first." The officer, whose name badge read Delancy, waved one of her colleagues over. "The kid's in the courthouse with Gloria Gannon. Go take a statement. I don't want the boy dragged back over here, but we're going to need Mrs. Gannon's side of the story."

The man began to stir at last, groaning, pushing glass off his chest. Paramedics arrived in an ambulance. They hurried over, but the other two police officers helped the would-be kidnapper to his feet, cuffed him and read him his rights.

While Daphne was telling Officer Delancy what she had seen, someone bolted from the courthouse. A broad arrow of pure fury, he headed straight for the guy in handcuffs.

"Where is she?" Patrick's voice cut through the crowd. "Where is she, you bastard? I'll kill you both with my bare hands if either of you comes near my child again."

Both Delancy and Daphne ran at the two men. The one in handcuffs struggled, wanting to get at

Patrick, and Patrick seemed willing to carry out his threat immediately.

"Mr. Gannon," Delancy said, "calm down. Everyone here will pretend we didn't hear that, and we'll all hope this guy won't remember it when next he's sober."

Daphne took Patrick's arm, all reticence gone. "Will's fine. He needs you free, not in jail for threatening this guy."

"I know Lisa sent him," Patrick said to the officers holding the men apart. "She'll send someone else. She has to be stopped, and if the system doesn't step up, I'll stop her—"

With all her strength, Daphne yanked him around. "Think about Will." She took possession of his gaze, knowing too well what could happen to the little boy if his father went to jail. "He's fine right now. He won't be if you get arrested."

"He's not fine." The rest of the square and all the low-voiced onlookers faded. Only she and Patrick were standing there, holding each other by the wrists. "His mother keeps trying to destroy any chance of a normal childhood for him, and I'm afraid she'll get him killed if she manages to take him away from me."

"So you need to make sure that doesn't happen. Look at that guy. He's hardly conscious."

"She sent him. You don't understand this situation, Daphne."

"And you're not going to dismiss me that easily. If your ex-wife is behind this, don't let her manipulate you into doing something that will give her Will."

"Mr. Gannon, this is a serious matter." Officer Delancy broke the spell. "Let us talk to this guy. If your wife is involved, we'll get the truth out of him, and she'll face charges, too. You know how this works."

"I know the custody agreement should have kept Will out of her hands, but this is the second time she's tried to take him."

"The second time?" Delancy asked.

"The first time she kept him after a visit. He was terrified by the time I found them—in Kentucky."

"Do you know this man? What's his name?"

"I don't know him, but who else would have sent him to grab my child?"

"Go back to Will. Comfort him. I may have to send a child services officer to talk to him. Ask your mother to come out here." Delancy started to walk away, but turned back. "Thank you, Miss Soder, we're done here." Her nod suggested Daphne go with Patrick.

What the hell? He needed someone and she cared about him. "I'm coming along, Patrick. I'd like to thank your mother."

He tugged his rumpled clothes into order. "Thank her for what?"

Daphne hurried to keep up with his worried stride. "She actually stopped him."

"She said you did, that she'd never have caught him if you hadn't gotten in front of him."

"I blocked his way," Daphne said. "But then I hesitated. Your mom sprinted over and clubbed him with a vase I was holding." Daphne looked back at the ruins on the ground and then at her open trunk.

Miriam would want to know about the wrecked floral arrangement and the others sitting out in the open.

"Why did you hesitate?" Anger simmered in the question.

"I told you. The guy's so strung out I'm surprised he made it through the grass without pitching Will on his head."

"You feel sorry for him?"

"Definitely not, but I doubt he'll remember anything when he sleeps it off."

"He'll remember Lisa."

"She'd be crazy to send someone as unreliable as he is. Doesn't it seem more likely this junkie wants drugs and saw a kid with an older, clearly affluent woman? Maybe he thought he could get money for Will."

"That would be too much of a coincidence."

"Fine, Patrick. I see you have this idea stuck in your head, but here's the truth. I'm worried about you and about Will."

He looked at her, his suffering as painful to her as if she were also a parent enduring the threat of danger to her child. "I am grateful you stopped him."

"With your mother." She could fight him, but his gratitude reminded her he didn't want her in his life. She turned her face from his. The little boy, who'd felt as shocked and frightened as a small animal in her arms, was in the revolving courthouse door. "Look. There's Will."

The door disgorged the child, and he ran into his father's arms. His eyes were wide, but he'd stopped crying.

"Let's go home, Daddy. I want to be home."

Will's small, tense voice scared Daphne.

"I need a few minutes, buddy. Maybe you could stay with Grandma while I get my things together?"

"I need to leave for a second." Gloria had joined them at a more sedate pace. "Maybe Daphne could keep an eye on Will if you need to go back upstairs."

Daphne took no offense at Patrick's obvious reluctance. "I understand," she said.

"No." He pulled himself together and reached for her. His hand grasped her shoulder firmly. He might not be willing to acknowledge the need that sharpened his face, but he couldn't hide it when he touched her. "Maybe you could come up to the courtroom. I need to guide my client through his allocution and finish the paperwork that will get him into treatment and off my desk."

Gloria looked taken aback.

Patrick grabbed at his tie. "Sorry. I'm not thinking clearly, or I wouldn't be shouting his business like the freaking town crier." He shut his mouth again, holding Will's head against him with a shaking hand. Daphne would have done anything to lessen his pain. "Can you come sit with Will for a few minutes outside the courtroom?"

"Sure. Do you mind, Will?"

Patrick's son lifted his head, and Patrick's face in miniature looked at her, blue eyes more scared than icy, his mouth almost curved in a hesitant smile.

"You made that man stop running with me," he said.

He owned her with his tiny voice and his acceptance. She'd been that child, who knew bad things happened and believed they might again. "Grandma did the hard work. Do you want to sit with me for a little while?"

"Maybe."

"I'll hurry." Gloria set out again at a pace that would have shamed a woman half her age. "And, Will, when I get back, you and Daddy and I are going to bake cookies at your house."

"Well, Daddy may write up a restraining order," Patrick said. "But I can do that after we make cookies if you want them, Will."

"I like 'em." Unconvinced, but willing to be persuaded, he plied Daphne with some Gannon charm. "You come, too, and make cookies."

Silence hit like a bomb. Daphne backpedaled first. "I'm sure your grandma and your dad—"

"We'd love to have you join us," Gloria said, over her shoulder. "Wouldn't we, Patrick?"

"Come make cookies," he said, but he seemed to be offering other pleasures.

"You sound funny, Daddy."

"I'm just so glad Grandma and Daphne kept you safe."

"She helped me get back to Grandma." Will clung to his father, shy and sweet. "So she can make cookies with us, right?"

Daphne trailed father and son inside and then into the lobby elevator. What next? As the car opened, Patrick turned left and hurried toward a set of highly varnished double doors.

He unpeeled Will's arms from around his neck and set him on a bench, pausing to kiss his boy's forehead. His long fingers, stroking Will's cheek, touched Daphne in a way totally different than when he'd held her. This was family. This was what she dreamed of, yet hardly dared to believe that the dream could come true.

She slid onto the bench and touched Patrick's arm, enjoying the silky brush of dark hair on his strong wrist. "I have to call Miriam. Can I use my cell out here?"

His gaze zeroed in on her. "You were supposed to be working?"

"It doesn't matter. I only want to let her know I'll come back to the shop later, and she'll need to redo that one arrangement."

Half a smile tilted his mouth. She held her breath, aware that he was able to reach her in a way nobody else had ever done before.

"I'll be back as soon as I can, bud." He ruffled Will's hair and then touched Daphne's shoulder again. She felt her whole body quiver. "Thank you," he said. "This little guy means the world to me."

Daphne fought tears. She put her arm around Will, and he leaned against her. His body, warm and trusting, curved into hers, made her tears fall. She closed her eyes, hoping he wouldn't see. There was no way to explain to a five-year-old that she wasn't sad. She was simply moved by Patrick's love for his son.

CHAPTER NINE

"MMM, DADDY." Will chomped on the first cookie, but then grabbed another one, fresh off the plate. "Give this one to Aunt Daphne. They're yummy, Aunt Daphne."

Gloria turned from pulling another tray out of the stove. "Maybe you could offer Daphne the plate."

Laughing, Patrick looked more relaxed than Daphne had ever seen him. He'd dropped his coat on a bench by the front door and rolled up his sleeves. Flour streaked his dark pants and stuck to his elbow.

He popped Will's offering into his mouth, but then came around the counter with the plate and a napkin. The closer he got, the less comfortable Daphne felt.

"I'm still loading this pan," she said, her hands full of big spoon and cookie dough. "I thought you said the oven shouldn't go empty until the cookies were all baked, Gloria."

"I just don't like to waste energy. Come help me wash this bowl, Will, honey."

At the sink, Will climbed onto a stool, talking to his grandmother about the cookies they'd just made. Patrick came to Daphne's side, a cookie in his hand. She looked into his eyes.

He didn't understand what she was about. She wanted this kind of life, an evening in a kitchen with family, a mother like Gloria, a child as full of trust and as beloved as Will obviously was.

But she also wanted Patrick, and he'd made his decision perfectly clear. Now, as he offered her an oatmeal cookie, his gaze was on her mouth as if they were alone.

"Do you want a bite?" he asked.

She glanced at his mother and son. "You don't seem sure of what you want."

"I'm offering you a cookie." The silence between them was loud with unspoken passion. He curved his index finger beneath her chin. "Open your mouth," he said.

"I'm not afraid." She caught his hand. "Are you?"

Patrick stroked her bottom lip. She gasped and he broke off a piece of cookie. Not quite as in control as she'd meant to be, she opened her mouth and he set the piece on her tongue. Only the cookie stopped her from following the pad of his finger as he stroked her again.

He curved his hand around her throat in a grazing, disturbing caress. She jerked away. He could talk about not getting involved, but he wasn't willing to let go, either.

"The cookies are wonderful, Gloria," she said.

Gloria turned just in time to miss Patrick turning a groan into a sigh.

Will jumped off his stool. "Are you hurt, Aunt Daphne? You sound funny."

"I'm fine, honey." Not hurt yet, but fully aware

that she was laying herself open to that possibility. Patrick might be worth it. Feelings this strong didn't come along every day.

"I'LL DRIVE YOU BACK to your car," Patrick said. Deep down he knew he'd wanted time alone with her since she'd accepted his mother and son's invitation to join them. "Mom, do you mind looking after Will?"

"Not a bit. Let's get started on bath time as soon as we pack up some cookies for Daphne."

"Okay, Grandma. Thanks for helping me today, Aunt Daphne."

"You're welcome." She leaned down and hugged him. Her dark brown hair mingled with his blond. Will's hands locked around her neck in a little boy's hug.

The room seemed to darken around them. If only he could trust that Daphne would never drink again. If only Will hadn't suffered already because his father had been blind to Lisa's addiction.

"You were very brave." Daphne dropped to her knees in front of Will. "And you did great."

"I was scared."

"Me, too, but because you yelled loudly, everything came out all right." She hugged him again. She'd obviously been around children. Patrick hadn't been so much at ease with his own son when he'd first started the divorce.

"I knew if my grandma heard me, she would catch him and make him let me go."

"You have the fastest grandma I've ever seen."

Daphne rose, and Gloria, smiling, handed her a plate wrapped in plastic.

"Thank you for everything," Patrick's mother said with meaning.

"I'm just glad I was able to help. Night, Gloria. Night, Will."

"Good night, son. I'll come kiss you when I get home."

"Okay, Daddy."

Daphne opened the kitchen door into the garden, and Patrick grabbed his coat and followed. In silence, she let him hold the gate for her. He hit the door locks on his keyless entry, and opened the passenger door.

"I'm sorry. I should have brought my own car," she said. "I wasn't thinking clearly."

"None of us was."

He shut the door and went around to the driver's side. Her scent filled his car.

His hands tightened on the keys. "I want to talk to you," he said.

"To tell me I'm not good enough because I'm fighting a drinking problem?"

"I don't know what I want to say. How do I explain you matter to me already? I've only known you a few weeks, but you make me feel as though I could care again."

"I feel the same, Patrick, and I never thought I would."

"But no matter how you make me feel, I have to remember that one day you could make a mistake, and your alcoholism could put my son in danger."

"No." As she shook her head, her hair whispered against the leather seat. "I could drink. I have to face that, but I know beyond any doubt that I would never hurt Will. Not just because he's a little boy who's already suffered enough for a lifetime, but also because he's your son. Part of you."

"Jeez, Daphne." She took his breath away. Suddenly, he felt as if he were in a room with no oxygen.

"Will you ever trust me enough to give me a chance, Patrick?"

He didn't answer, and she didn't pursue the subject. He had a feeling men had treated her badly in the past. She understood how that worked, but she didn't understand that he was fighting for his son—to make sure his choices didn't hurt Will again.

They reached the square and her car. Daphne gathered her keys from the soft shoulder bag she carried.

"Thanks for the ride."

"Daphne?"

"Don't." She turned without opening the door. "I'm not playing games. I've never been good at pretending feelings don't matter."

"Are you kidding?" He put his hand on the console between them. "Relationships are rarely as simple as a man and a woman deciding to be together. There are usually other factors."

"Such as?"

"Lisa and me. I thought I loved her enough to keep her and Will safe. But I was wrong. Now, every time I think of her, I see my son lethargic and damn near dead in the back of that car. I don't know if I'll ever be able to say her name again without wanting to hurt someone."

"You're not allowed to hurt me because of her. You want me. I think I even need you. I could be the answer to your prayers, but you're too afraid to reach for me."

Swearing, he did just that, to keep her from opening the door and walking away again. He pulled her as close as the car would allow, and holding her nearly made him believe she was right. Her gaze, intent on his mouth, both challenged and pleaded.

"I can't," he said, mostly to himself.

"Why not? Why let something that will never happen ruin your life? Because losing me might be that bad, Patrick."

The console bit into his ribs. She stared into his eyes, hers all passion in the streetlights.

"Kiss me, Patrick, and mean it. Know that it won't be the last time."

She caught the sides of his jacket and pulled him so close he had only to breathe to take her mouth.

"Are you safe, Daphne? Am I making a mistake that could hurt my son?"

"You'd be crazy if you weren't wary, but I've felt all your doubts about myself. I wouldn't pretend if I didn't think I could stay sober. When are you going to change and show Will how to get over being afraid?"

She caught his face in her hands, but he couldn't fight. He was already kissing her. The instant she opened to him, he felt as if he was sliding off the edge of fear. All that mattered was being close to this woman, touching her, pleasing her, healing himself in the passion of her need.

A warning voice screamed inside his head as he fought its power. She wanted him and he wanted her. Wasn't that reason enough?

Did he dare trust that she would never hurt his son? With a groan, he pulled her closer still, tried to drive the doubts out of his own mind.

His hands fell down her shoulders. She pulled back, opening the cardigan that made her skin glow as if a fire lay inside her. She undid the top button of her dress. He took the second.

"Don't rip them," she said between caressing his jawline with her mouth. "I'm poor, remember."

He laughed in answer to the laughter in her voice.

A rap at the window stilled them both and brought reality back with a thud. He helped her button her dress, his fingers trembling against the full breasts that taunted his sleep.

The second rap was a thud.

"Cops?" Daphne yanked her sweater together. "Open the window before you're all over the evening news. I don't want your mother or Will seeing this."

"Or Raina."

"She'd be fine. She'd laugh at us."

She was wrong. When he put the window down, Raina stood outside on the curb, and she wasn't laughing.

In jeans and a T-shirt and pearls, she looked conventional—and furious. "What are you thinking? The windows are smoked. This street is empty. I could have been any lunatic."

There was no way he could get out of the car just now to reassure her. "I'll explain later, Raina. You're absolutely right."

"Daphne, get out of the car."

Daphne burst into laughter. "It's all right, Raina."

"I heard what happened on the square today. I had to hear from gossip, and I guess I'll be hearing about this from the same source because Mrs. Tandred still rents that apartment above the bookstore."

"Will's fine." Daphne leaned across Patrick. Her breast, jutting into his shoulder, didn't help his situation any.

"You idiot, I've been worried about you, too. Mrs. Tandred thought you were me, and she said you were nearly hit by a car—"

"What car?" Patrick asked, sliding his hand down her back. "Did you get hurt?"

"You've had your turn to ask, but you were apparently after other information from my sister."

"Raina, you're overreacting," Daphne said.

"Get out of the car," Raina said again. "And you're not staying in that fleabag hotel another night. I nearly lost my mind when I couldn't reach you. Where is your phone?"

Daphne felt around for it. "In my car, I guess."

"I'm taking you to the hotel and you're packing and coming home with me."

"I'm not. Calm down."

"You are, if I have to pack for you."

"Let's talk rent," Daphne said.

"Are you both kidding me?" Patrick asked.

Daphne grinned at him. "I've got her cornered. She's angry and scared right now. Tomorrow she's just going to be pissed."

"Funny. Patrick, can you take your hands off my sister before you get her arrested? Daphne, we have ordinances in this town and you'll find yourself all over the front page. Which will land on Patrick's front door first thing in the a.m., and I happen to know their ritual is for Will to grab the paper while Patrick makes breakfast."

"You're right." Daphne crawled back onto her side of the car and opened the door.

Patrick scrambled out of his side, aware of both women, his friend and his almost-lover. Raina looked as if she wanted to kill him.

"I have to go," Daphne said. "We should talk."

"So are you moving in with Raina?"

"If we agree on rent," she said, looking at her sister with determination.

"Whatever you want," Raina said. "I'll steal you blind if I don't have to worry about you anymore. Good night, Patrick."

"Hold on." Raina's attitude was starting to bug him. He wasn't about to be treated like the flotsam in her sister's life. "I'll come to the house tomorrow, Daphne."

"You have my cell number."

"A fat lot of good that did me," Raina said. She

took her sister's arm and hauled her toward Daphne's battered car. "What possessed you to go after that guy in the square? And then not call me? I thought he might have friends who'd come after you."

Daphne looked back, but Patrick was remembering Will. That guy might have friends, and one of them might be Lisa. He had to make sure his son was safe before he made love to a woman in public again.

"WHY DID YOU NEED to see her?" his mother asked with the foyer light behind her as he let himself into his house.

"She helped us. I had to thank her."

"I think there's more. I sensed something between you."

She'd have been blind if she hadn't. He shook his head. "Don't worry about it, Mom." He scooped her sweater off the bench near the door. "Where did you park?"

"I'll be fine. Will's restless. Be quiet when you go upstairs." She put on her sweater, brushing his hands away. "Stop helping everyone else, and think about yourself. You've been divorced for over a year."

"I never know when Lisa or someone she's hired is going to make a grab for my son."

"If she won't get treatment, you can't change Will's situation. Do you plan to spend the rest of your life barring the door?"

"Until Will can protect himself." He opened the door for her. "What choice do I have?"

She buttoned her collar with a heavy sigh. "None,

but you're my son, and I see that woman tying you and Will up in knots. To tell you the truth, I could use a vase and a shot at her head, too."

He hugged her, one-armed. "She's changing us all, Mother. That's what bothers me most. How many more times will this happen before my son refuses to set foot out of the house? And here you are, a pacifist, looking to brain her."

"I no longer believe her story about not having a problem."

"Did you ever?"

"I thought she believed it. She has to realize something's wrong if she's willing to send a guy who shouldn't be out of a jail cell to bring her son to whatever hole she calls home now."

"Good night." He couldn't let himself look at images of Will in a filthy room with Lisa and her ever-spiraling sickness. "And we don't actually know for sure she arranged a kidnapping. I assumed it."

"With reason."

His mother gave up lecturing and headed into the night. He watched her get in her car and drive away. Then he locked the doors and set the alarm.

The stairs seemed endless as he climbed toward Will. Would the cops find Lisa through her accomplice? He walked into his son's room.

He'd painted the bedroom wall with airplanes and balloons. Amateurish, but Will loved them. From the first time a jet had passed overhead on its way to Reagan National, Will had strained toward it from his baby carriage.

Good thing Patrick wasn't looking to share a family-law office with his son. If Will wasn't a pilot-in-training, no one was.

Will rolled over and held out his arms. "Where's my Airbus, Dad?"

"Here, buddy." He picked it up from the floor. Once upon a long time ago, Lisa had cut and assembled a cloth Airbus and stuffed it to keep Will from poking his eye out with his plastic one while he was sleeping. Patrick tucked it into the crook of Will's arm. "Night, son."

"Daddy?"

"Huh?"

Will flung his free arm over his head. "I miss my mommy."

"I know, bud, and she misses you, too." The reassurance made him feel as if he'd swallowed poison. "Everything will be all right."

"Okay."

With a heavy heart, he turned down the dimmer on Will's light switch. Ever since the divorce, Will was afraid of total darkness. Today wouldn't change that for the better.

The pediatrician said it was natural because his world had changed. For Patrick, it was a lot more specific. He and his son had learned there were monsters in the dark.

He started toward his own room, but a knot of fear dragged him back. He lay down beside Will, who curled into his body.

How would it be if he could lie here until Will's

nearness convinced him it was safe to go to his own room? And then in his bed, to find someone like Daphne—hell, to find Daphne—waiting for him? Wanting him with passion uncomplicated by fear and mistrust?

It couldn't happen.

Even if his son were safe, would he or Will ever feel secure again? He stroked his boy's hair away from his face and then kissed his temple.

And eventually, after his mind stopped working at a frenetic pace, Patrick fell asleep.

"I DON'T GIVE A DAMN about Patrick right now." Raina opened her front door and reached back for one of Daphne's bags, which she flung into the front hall.

"Maybe he needs to relax once in a while," Daphne said. "I don't think he's detached as he wants to be."

"Are you willing to let him use you?"

Daphne tossed the rest of her things into Raina's hall, as well, sobering at last. "He's your best friend. Why would you think he'd use me?"

Raina shut the wide door in silence. Immediately, the shadows gathered around them, and Daphne felt the house's emptiness.

"I know how afraid he is," Raina said, calmer at last. "Will is his priority, Daphne, and you don't strike me as being naive."

"I'm not."

"Then how do you explain tonight? How would

you have felt if I was some cop? You have to know that your face would have been all over the paper because Patrick and I are news in this one-paper town."

"Are you worried because my face is also yours?"

"I'm worried because you did a reckless thing this afternoon, helping Gloria knock that guy down, and then tonight you were downright courting disaster. Patrick blames Lisa for everything that's happened to Will. He's reluctant to be with you because you're fighting an addiction. When you're not sitting in his lap, he's going to remember why he was unwilling to be with you."

"You sound like one of my foster mothers," Daphne said, and then held up her hands as Raina looked disgusted. "I put that wrong, but she always said men were out for one thing. It's not that simple, but you are right. He will remember, and I will be the bad woman again."

"Then what were you thinking?"

"I *have* been a bad woman." She went to the duffel where she hoped to find pajamas. "I've wanted safety more than anything else in the world. I understand Patrick's instincts."

"Even if they're designed specifically to hurt you?"

"I'll protect myself in the end, Raina. I won't let him hurt me, but I'm feeling confident these days. I have you, and Miriam values me as a friend and an employee. Tonight was a nice night with good friends after something terrifying happened."

"So you and Patrick were simply reacting to fear for Will?" Raina opened a zip-up tote and yanked out pajamas and toothpaste and a toothbrush. "You are so disorganized."

"I'm happy." Daphne caught her hand. "Because you accepted me, you made me start believing in myself, and I can't go back. I won't. You don't need to worry."

"I love Patrick," Raina said, "but you're my sister."

Daphne hugged her. "Thanks for the room."

"Sure. Sorry I was so—"

"Bossy?" Daphne suggested with a grin.

Raina's laugh matched the weary set of her shoulders. "You're kind. Are you hungry? Thirsty?"

"Ready for bed, if you'll show me where it is."

"Let's leave your stuff here. We can deal with it tomorrow."

CHAPTER TEN

SECOND THOUGHTS KEPT Patrick from doing the right thing the next night and for twenty-some nights after that. He never contacted Daphne as they'd agreed. As he turned on his son's night-light, he told himself he was being fair to her. Those moments in the car had changed their relationship and he didn't want to hurt her.

She wasn't just a woman who made him want sex. She wasn't like Lisa, some symbol of a wasted life that could put his son in the back of another freezing car.

Daphne made him feel easier in his own skin. If not for Will, he'd have been unwilling to let her go, even with Raina.

But he did have Will, and Daphne had a past she didn't try to hide. Her problems kept her going to a church most nights for a meeting of people who no longer wanted to ruin their lives with addiction.

Patrick went to his own room. His house was clean. His ritual was safe. His son slept down the hall, in part because Daphne had put herself in the way of Danny Frank, a junkie who'd refused in the past three weeks to admit he even knew Lisa.

Patrick wasn't as worried about Danny Frank. If he had a connection with Lisa, the police would find it, and her visitations with their son would be so restricted she'd never find the energy to carry through on the judge's instructions to get treatment.

His worry now was Daphne and his own ungovernable need. He'd been an attorney for a lot of years. She'd admitted to questionable behavior, but he needed dry facts without the emotion of sharing all the terrified moments she'd experienced in her life. He was hurting her and killing himself with his silence.

Confirming the facts she'd shared, and learning more details was as simple as turning on the computer. Someone would have kept a record of a young woman who'd passed from foster home to foster home.

He had no right to search. She'd revealed the part of her life she'd wanted him to know.

Patrick went downstairs to his office in the back of the narrow house and turned on the computer. It whirred and clicked.

He took a note from his desk drawer, the copy Daphne had sent to his office when she'd confirmed the time and date for her first meeting with Raina. Patrick stared at her name.

Love had been missing from his life for a long time. Passion was a dim memory that haunted more than comforted.

Until Daphne.

Why couldn't he just accept what she'd said? Why couldn't he believe she'd never hurt Will?

Staring at her note, he was struck. There was a reason he'd found only track-and-field results when he'd searched for Daphne Sodar. He'd spelled her last name wrong.

Patrick stared from the note to his computer, up and running, humming in anticipation of a little work.

He could let it all go. Concentrate on Will and work and recovering a livable life.

Or he could believe Daphne. Accept her version of everything and let the rest of the world go hang. Except the biggest part of his world lay upstairs, already a victim of his father's bad judgment.

Swearing, Patrick tapped out Daphne's name and the birth date he knew because he'd known her twin all her life. Several hits rolled up.

A sealed juvenile record. His gut tightened, and he pushed back.

It shouldn't be a big surprise. She'd told him and he'd been startled to find nothing. But seeing it in black and white… Knowing that Lisa had come from a good family and a fine education and still couldn't control the need that was ruining her life…

Patrick had come to the bar believing humans learned the difference between right and wrong and knew how to choose a path that caused the least harm.

But he'd been so blind he hadn't seen the harm and neglect in his own home. The divorce had peeled the self-congratulatory film from his eyes. These days, while he'd ached for his son, he'd also found more sympathy for clients.

The pattern was right there on his monitor screen,

an incident that required police intervention, followed by periods of quiet. Trouble and redemption.

What chance would Daphne have of staying out of trouble? With only her own instincts—loving, kind, courageous instincts—to support her she might easily succumb.

He twisted his neck, his skin crawling at the thought of Daphne facing a cop, having chosen badly from her few options.

"Damn it. Who the hell am I to judge?"

He wasn't even decent enough to turn his back on the electronic trail of Daphne's history.

He scrolled through the records on his monitor, the criminology degree, her success as a jury consultant. A phenomenal record. He'd have hired her in a heartbeat.

A few screens later, her name came up in Milton Stegwell's case. Daphne's instincts had abandoned her. She'd believed the bastard. Four months later, Daphne had been arrested for driving under the influence.

That had been a year ago. Nothing more showed on her record. She'd told him everything there was to discover. But was this the calm before her next storm?

Patrick pushed back his chair again, his stomach heaving.

SLEEP? It seemed to be avoiding her again.

This wasn't her kind of place, a mansion on a hill clinging like a vulture to the side of a Virginia mountain. She'd given in too easily.

Being rescued wasn't her kind of choice.

She eased out of the massive suite across from her sister's room. The wide stairs, almost as wide as one of the town's winding roads, creaked as she tiptoed down them.

She found the library and searched for a book on the towering shelves. Raina had lent her *David Copperfield* already, and the rest of the Charles Dickens set was waiting, but they were all so perfectly arranged, in such mint condition, highly prized.

Tonight, feeling vulnerable and lost—because a man had avoided her since the night they'd feverishly torn at each other's clothes—she couldn't make herself pull another volume down. She could get her books from the public library and avoid the worry of marring the pristine Abernathy books. She didn't belong here.

Patrick wasn't her only problem. After all, she could tell him he needed her until she was blue in the face, but she understood she couldn't *make* him feel safe with her. She loved living with Raina, loved her new, quiet life in Honesty, and the certainty that she was making good on all the promises she'd made after the DUI incident.

But she was sheltering in safety. She had to live again, choose a future, not wait for it to come her way. Maybe she'd been hoping Patrick would love her and take away the responsibility of making choices.

She turned toward the windows and nearly walked into the liquor cabinet. Cut glass glittered, flashing the rich colors of the drink inside.

Daphne licked her lips.

God, a drink would taste good. Would feel good. She clenched her hands behind her back.

"Daph?"

She whirled. Raina, dazed with sleep, stood in the doorway. An angel in the nick of time.

"What are you doing?" she asked.

"I've never had a nickname."

"Daphne took too long. I'm dead on my feet, but I must have heard you come down here. Are you okay?"

"I'm fine." Better especially since her sister was between her and the liquor cabinet.

"Did you have a nightmare?" Clinging to the door frame, her hair falling in strands over her shoulders, Raina opened one eye. "Are you—" That question, she didn't finish, but she didn't have to when her gaze twitched to the abundant supply of booze. "What are you doing?"

"Going back to bed." She wouldn't thank her sister for saving her because she didn't want Raina to think she always turned to a bottle when she felt lost.

"Wait for me." Raina caught the light switch and followed Daphne up the stairs. "You have to work tomorrow."

"Uh-huh. That might be the answer."

"What?"

"Nothing."

"I think you need sleep. I hear you walking around at night."

"I'll be okay."

"Night," Raina said at her room.

"Good night."

Daphne closed the bedroom door behind herself and walked the mile it took to reach her borrowed bed. She climbed in, enjoying the texture of sheets that must have an astronomical thread count. She resisted pulling them over her head.

Tomorrow she'd start a new résumé. Patrick and selling flowers and a couple of months of no pressure had been a nice diversion, but it was time to face real life.

DAPHNE LEFT EARLY to work on her résumé at the library's computers. With the file nicely begun, she stopped for a vat of strong coffee on her way to work.

Thanks in part to Raina, she'd avoided temptation, but she felt as if she had the hangover anyway. She'd learned to be around alcohol. She had friends who drank and to expect them to abstain in front of her would have been ridiculous. But when the need came back, as it had last night, it terrified her.

At the shop she pushed through the door and proved the maxim that eavesdroppers hear no good about themselves.

"I don't care what you say, Miriam. There's something funny about a woman who comes to town practically the day her doppelganger buries her mother."

"You don't know what's between Raina Abernathy and Daphne Soder. Neither do I. What I know is that she works hard and takes on more work than I expected when I placed that ad, and I'm happy to have her. Now, if you want an arrangement, I'll be glad to make it, but if you insult my employee and make her leave me high and dry, I'm going to be angry."

"You're my cousin, Miriam. Don't act like this isn't my business."

"Until you start signing my mortgage checks, I'm not acting."

She walked into the main shop, all but herding an older woman toward the door. The woman's perfect taupe linen suit proclaimed her one of Raina's crowd. Daphne walked to the counter and pulled out an apron.

"We should apologize," Miriam said.

"It's okay." Daphne had expected worse from the moment she'd parked that first day. "I'll start sweeping in the back."

"This is my cousin, Elaine Havers. Elaine, Daphne. My friend," she said with extra emphasis.

Elaine held out her hand. "Nice to meet you. I know Raina well."

Daphne left the bait in the water. "I'll tell her you said hello." She shook the woman's hand, smiled as brightly as she could while someone played a cracked Liberty Bell in her head and marched past the two women, grabbing a broom along the way.

The bell over the door tinkled, and then footsteps came back. She didn't look up.

"I wanted to talk to you anyway," Miriam said.

"It's fine. Everyone keeps reminding me this is a small town. I'm happy to provide entertainment."

"Not about my nutty cousin. You're doing more work than I'm paying you for. I need to give you a raise."

Daphne paused with the broom jammed under a shelf of orchids. "You don't have to bribe me because your cousin was rude."

"It's no bribe. Just bad timing. Let's consider it done."

"Actually, I needed to talk to you."

"You're quitting?"

Daphne laughed, although she felt guilty because Miriam looked stricken. "I'm not leaving, but I am going to start advertising for my old job."

"I love Elaine, but sometimes I can't stand her," Miriam said. "She always judges people by the cars they drive, the clothes they wear. She'd never dare talk to Raina like that."

"It's not Elaine. I've been feeling as if I needed to do this. Honesty is a small town and I probably won't find cases right away. I may never find a steady stream of work, so I'll be grateful for a steady paycheck here if you don't mind my doing both. It would mean a change in schedule sometimes."

"We'll work around it. You're sure you're not letting Elaine push you out of here?"

"Not a chance." She swept a couple of feet, raising more dust than she was collecting. Her hand trembled on the broom. Funny how making the right decision could shake a woman. "Do you mind if I take a long lunch today?"

"I probably owe you time."

THAT LUNCH-HOUR MEETING might have saved her life. She'd been on a little vacation, but she came out of the bowels of the church feeling as if she had a grip again.

Until she ran into Gloria Gannon, coming down the same stairs where she'd run into Raina weeks ago.

She slammed her hand against her stomach, feeling sick. She cared what Gloria thought of her, not just because she was one of the world's "nice" women, but because she mattered to Patrick.

"Morning," Gloria said. "I've been wondering when we'd see you again. How have you been?"

"Fine." She smoothed her jeans, touched her hair, plucked at the scooped collar of her tulip-printed T-shirt. Anything to distract Gloria from the hallway downstairs. Gloria was not distractible.

"Oh," she said after a few moments, clearly leaping to the correct conclusion.

Somehow, she disappointed Daphne. Being considered a barely functioning alcoholic went a long way toward curing shame. The fine people of Honesty were starting to get on her nerves. Did she have to run into everyone she knew in the space of one morning?

"You're right in what you're thinking," she said. "Mostly. I've had a problem. I may still have a problem, but I'm aware and fighting it. I'm no danger to Raina."

"This is why Patrick's avoiding you."

Daphne tried to pretend she didn't care. She failed. "He thinks I'll drink again. He thinks I won't be able to help it and I may hurt Will."

"You two have covered a lot of ground," Gloria said. "Is he in love with you?"

Daphne shook her head, refusing to give in to

stinging tears. "We've been over this ground because of Will. You have to talk about the important things early when a child's involved."

Gloria came down another couple of steps. Empathy made her beautiful. Her smile almost gave Daphne hope. "You may be wrong about Patrick."

Gloria might be wise and strong, but she didn't know her own son.

"I'm not."

AT LAST CAME the day they delivered Hal safely to the county jail, where one of the local psychologists would provide a course of anger management therapy. Patrick tried to concentrate on the next cases going to court.

Work had always been his refuge. He'd lost himself so thoroughly in work he'd managed to believe Lisa's excuses for forgotten appointments, falls that made no sense for a young woman of sound body, even two car accidents she'd blamed on her well-treated "nerves."

Today, he couldn't focus on his clients. In the back of his mind, Daphne waited. A smile, a twitch of her pale orange sundress. A series of truths she'd already told him that he'd uncovered in black and white.

He'd give anything to make it stop mattering.

The phone on his desk rang. It was his private line and when he answered, Sheriff Tom Drake identified himself.

"I want to talk to you about Danny Frank," he said.

"My ex-wife hired him?"

"Actually, we heard from Lisa. She has an attorney and she sent an affidavit, along with a recording from her voice mail. Frank did it for her, but she had no knowledge of his actions."

"What?"

"She broke off their relationship and he wanted to win her back. He thought stealing her kid might do the trick."

"God. You're positive she didn't talk him into it?"

"She spent most of the conversation begging me to tell her Will wasn't going to be marked for life. I told her he seems to be coping well."

"What happens next?"

"Frank goes to trial, but I thought you'd want to know about Lisa."

"Thanks, Tom."

"I guess she might be changing after all."

"Yeah." It was the most frightening thing she'd done yet.

"What will happen with Frank now?"

"As I said, he'll go to trial."

"And jail?"

"I hope so."

"Thanks, Tom."

He called his mother to let her know. Her wary "Hey, Patrick" alarmed him.

"Is something wrong with Will?" He went to the window where spring sunshine over the courthouse blinded him. Covering his eyes, he turned back to the sun-spotted, orderly confines of his office. He'd talked to his son while his mother had driven Will back to her house and he'd been okay.

"He's fine. We made Play-Doh after school. I have

the biggest pretzel in the whole wide world on my kitchen table."

His sigh of relief was ridiculous. He had to put his life in order. "Tom Drake just called me." He filled her in.

"Have you called Daphne?"

He stared at his phone. "Daphne?"

"Don't get all defensive. She was part of this, too, and you should let her know."

Why bother trying to persuade her he didn't care about Daphne? "I'll call her."

"Good. I think you need to talk."

"What's going on, Mother?"

"With me? Nothing. Talk to you later."

He dialed Daphne's cell phone. She answered after several rings.

"Patrick?"

"I don't blame you for being surprised. I should have called you."

"I guessed you'd decided what you wanted from us."

"I didn't decide," he said. "I've been longing for you like a schoolkid and wishing I weren't too afraid for Will to come to you."

"Have you ever thought you may be using Will as a shield?"

"He's my son."

Silence went both ways over the line.

"The Sheriff—Tom Drake—called me a few minutes ago," Patrick finally said. "Lisa knew this Danny Frank, but she didn't put him up to kidnapping Will. Apparently, he felt he was doing her a favor."

"They're certain?"

"She taped something off her voice mail that puts her in the clear."

"How are you?"

"About that? I'm worried. It sounds as if she's in a sober moment if she managed to get her evidence together. I'm thinking she may come back for Will."

"If she could sober up it might be best. He needs his mother."

"People say that, but they don't know…"

"I know," she said.

"That's why I stopped. You do know how it's been for him, or you know something similar. But I don't want him to endure the childhood you had."

"He has you," she said with generosity he didn't deserve.

"I love him, Daphne. More than anything."

"I know." She was silent a moment. "I've been meaning to call you, too. I'm starting to look for work as a jury consultant again, so you'll see me around the courthouse."

"Are you ready for that?"

"I have to live again. I can't hide forever." Implicit was the truth. He was happy to hide, and he was if it kept Will safe.

"Do you want to drop your résumé by here?"

"No, thanks. I just wanted to warn you you'll see me in the courthouse."

"I'd be glad to take your information, Daphne."

"I don't want to work with you," she said, "and I'm sorry to cut this short, but I'm outside the shop and Miriam is waiting for me to make a couple of deliveries."

She hung up. He stared at the phone. Lisa's anger had never left him in any doubt. If Daphne was angry, she hid it well, but she'd talked to him as if she hardly knew him. Maybe she didn't want to know him anymore.

Maybe she'd finally taken him at his word and moved on.

He shut the phone with a slap and stood. Familiar sights outside the window provided no relief. He turned for the door and almost passed his assistant without speaking.

"Mr. Gannon?"

"I'm going out."

"You'll be back?"

"Probably not. If anyone calls with an urgent problem, leave me a voice mail. I'll check in later."

He was charging down the sidewalk, apologizing right and left, when he saw Daphne driving away from Miriam's store.

He laughed at himself. What could he have expected? And why the hell was he chasing her down when pretending wasn't fair to her, either? He had an early afternoon. He'd spend it with Will.

HIS MOTHER ANSWERED the door, surprised. "Come in. We're baking our footprints."

"You should have been a kindergarten teacher yourself," he said.

"I am creative." She seemed to be talking without

thinking. She eyed him as if she were looking for signs of smallpox.

"Daddy, look."

Will ran down the hall carrying several wads of dough, jammed together to sort of resemble an airplane. A couple of pieces flopped onto his grandmother's pristine parquet floor, and he stopped, stomping them into the wood as he tried to pick them up.

"Uh-oh," he said, tripping until Patrick hurried to catch him by the sticky elbows. "My nose wheels."

"We can put that back together," Patrick said.

They made bugs and dogs and cats and a Cessna out of the world's largest pretzel and ate dinner, and then Patrick and Will bent their heads over Will's ABCs while Gloria spooned clotted cream over warm apple crisp.

Afterward, Patrick helped his son pack his things.

"Kiss Grandma goodbye."

She bent and Will jumped and they head-butted.

"Sorry, Grandma." Will rubbed his head. "That smarted."

"For me, too."

Gloria kissed his boo-boo, while Patrick inspected for concussion. Single parenthood had turned him into a regular grandma himself, which was nothing a man might brag about.

"I'll see you both tomorrow," his mother said as she walked them to the door.

"Thanks for everything," Patrick said.

"Notice I haven't asked for an explanation?"

"I got so wound up in your big baked footprints I forgot to notice."

She mocked him with a fake "Heh heh." Then she kissed Will again and caught Patrick's arm. "You be careful, you hear me?"

"Subtle, Mom. What's up?"

"Nothing." She took a deep breath and ruffled Will's hair. "See you, guys."

Halfway to the car, Will held up his arms. "Carry me, Daddy."

They waved goodbye again, and Gloria finally turned away. Patrick helped Will in and got behind the wheel.

At the red light by the square, they hit a traffic jam. Cars inched forward, their drivers particularly harassed and quick on the horn. Traffic jams in Honesty were almost nonexistent.

Will had begun to nod off, but the honking woke him. "What's wrong, Daddy?"

"Bunch of cars ahead, buddy. You can go back to sleep."

"I wasn't sleeping."

A battered white sedan was nosed to the corner of Main and Square. With its hood propped open, it exhaled a plume of steam. Patrick recognized it before he saw Daphne, studying the engine in consternation as the warm breeze feathered her hair around her neck.

She stepped out of a spreading pool of water in front of the grille. Her car hadn't just run hot. She'd cracked her radiator.

Immediately searching for a parking spot, Patrick

glanced at Will, who stretched as tall as he could manage in his seat.

"Aunt Raina?" Will pointed. "Why's Aunt Raina stuck with that car? That's not her car."

"That's Aunt Daphne."

"Let's help her, Dad."

Patrick's palms began to sweat on the steering wheel. He'd pulled away. They hadn't seen each other in almost a month. Going back, no matter how much he craved the mere scent of her skin, was wrong.

But he stared at her, a dying man in sight of salvation. Her flushed face might be due to heat or humiliation. Another car horn bleated and she turned, so tragically apologetic he wanted nothing more than to get out and teach the other driver manners.

Helping her wouldn't make her a part of his family, but he didn't want to stop at helping her. He wanted to hold her and feel her need racing with his.

"How about we call a tow truck?" Cursing himself, he picked up his cell phone.

"No, Daddy. I wanna help Aunt Daphne."

Patrick closed the phone. Even without Will's plea, he wouldn't have been able to drive past Daphne.

They drew even with her. The faint pink on her skin turned deep red.

He stopped the car and opened the doors so that Will wouldn't overheat. "We'll help Aunt Daphne make her deliveries."

Around him, the square erupted in a symphony of angry horns and shouts and a couple of colorful names he hoped Will wasn't hearing.

CHAPTER ELEVEN

"LET ME HELP YOU," PATRICK said, coming around his car, looking about as happy as Daphne felt.

The four words in the English language most perfectly designed to make her cut off her nose to spite her face.

If Miriam's afternoon deliveries weren't wilting in the backseat, for the second time since she'd taken this job, she might have walked away and never looked at the whole mess again.

"Move that heap out of the way."

Nodding, she waved her heckler on. "I'm fine, Patrick. I've just been trying to find a tow truck that can come now."

"I have a friend who charges fifty a tow. Do you want me to call him?"

She looked down at the fluid escaping from her radiator. "I'm going to need him anyway."

"Okay, but I'll help you deliver the flowers."

"Thanks." She pointed toward the car. "Is Will in there?" She saw his head wobbling as he strained to see over the high backseat of his father's car.

"Go say hi," Patrick said. "I'll call Kent and move the flowers."

"Thanks."

"No problem," he said, and his eyes roamed her face like a starving man's.

She ducked inside his car. Will held out his arms. "Aunt Daphne," he said. "Your car broke."

"It sure did."

"Daddy will fix it."

"Daddy is fixing it. I'm lucky you guys came along."

"He was going to call a tow truck, but I made him stop."

Daphne wasn't surprised. Naturally, he wouldn't want to help. He'd managed to hide from his feelings for a long time. Being dragged face-to-face with a woman who could make him live again had to be a shock.

Dolt.

"Well, I'm glad you were looking out for me." She kissed the top of his head. "You smell like bread."

"We made hands and feet." He pointed to a small stack of wax paper-covered objects. "See?"

"Awfully nice."

Orange and white lights turned onto Main Street, heading their way.

"There's your daddy's friend with his truck. I'd better go. Are you okay?"

"Sure. We're going to help you deliver your flowers."

"I'm looking forward to that."

Standing, she shaded her eyes, but she could catch

only glimpses of the orange lights between the traffic and the interested bystanders. Inch by inch, the vehicles took turns creeping past in both directions, allowing the lights to come closer and closer.

At last. Blessed towing equipment took shape behind the lights.

Relief made her a little dizzy.

"That's the last of the flowers." Patrick came to her side.

Nodding, she tiptoed for a glimpse of the tow truck's driver. His face was all concentration as he inched around her car and blocked another lane and a half.

"Will said you didn't want to stop."

"I didn't want to start anything up again," he said.

"You're a coward."

She went toward the truck. The door opened and her fairy godfather stepped out in greasy blue overalls and a red ball cap. According to the evidence of an embroidered white patch on his chest, he was indeed Patrick's friend.

"Kent, I have to declare my undying love for you."

His grin turned a little wary. Perhaps she'd gone too far. "Hey," he said. "Hey, Patrick."

"Hi, Kent. Thanks for coming so fast." They shook hands and then Patrick turned to her. "This is Daphne Soder."

"Hey, Daphne."

They shook hands, too, and then Patrick rested his hand on the hot metal of the fallen vehicle. "And this is her car."

"Yeah?" Kent arrowed his body over her engine

to more closely admire her busted radiator. "This thing won't ever move again without a tow."

"I was afraid of that." She reached into the driver's window for her purse. Her insurance card said nothing about towing. Swearing under her breath, she rifled her wallet. "How much will this cost?"

"Usually, fifty a tow," Kent said, "but I'm just hauling her about three blocks, so let's say thirty."

"You wouldn't want to say twenty-five?"

Patrick moved forward, clearly about to offer monetary assistance, too. Daphne stopped him with a look that somehow made him smile in surprise.

Someone honked again. Several drivers leaned on their horns in reply. Kent tipped the rim of his cap, sliding it back to reveal dirty-blond hair. "You seen gas prices lately?"

"Yeah, okay." She hated using her credit card. D-e-b-t also spelled insecurity.

He offered his hand again. "Deal at thirty?"

She shook it. "Deal. Do you know the folks who'll do the work on the car?"

"That'd also be me, ma'am." He pointed to his name as if she might have missed it. "You won't find a better price in town. Ask Patrick."

"I have plenty to ask Patrick." She turned back to her heap. First things first. "But I'm sorry for being so cranky with you. Do you know where I can rent a car?"

"We provide a loaner. It's not a luxury—" He broke off, surveying her rust-bucket chariot. "I guess you won't mind that, though."

Even Daphne had to laugh. "You can't imagine how grateful I am. I need my job if I'm going to pay you."

"Well, ma'am, let's get moving then."

IN THE END, Daphne asked Patrick to transfer the arrangements from his trunk to the loaner's trunk and she went on her way to make her deliveries. She'd thanked him, but he'd sensed her anger. Her impatience?

He tried not to think as he readied Will's clothes for the next morning and checked they'd done the right homework. The king of ABCs and colors in his kindergarten class, Will liked to have the correct answers. One day of his son's near hysteria because they'd done the wrong day's work had made him extra careful about getting the date and assignment combo right.

In the bathtub, Will was delivering color commentary as he dive-bombed plastic carriers with his fighters, which he could name by model. Patrick went to haul him and his boats out of the cooling water. "You have about two minutes."

"I'm not ready, Daddy. I'm doing a battle."

"You're crazy for planes, buddy."

Will slicked back his pale hair. "Once upon a day, I'll fly planes like these, Daddy."

"I'll be first in line for a ride."

"If I have room. Mommy doesn't want a ride. She doesn't want me to be a pilot."

For Will's sake, Patrick managed to hide his anger with Lisa. Shading the truth might not be honest, but Will needed some kind of mother figure. "Mommies worry about their boys. She wants you to be safe on the ground, at home."

"She's not home." Will's next bomb landed with even more force. "I don't get to be with both of you no more. Ever again."

He couldn't say, "Because your mommy might have gotten you killed."

"Sometimes that happens when people don't manage to make marriage work, buddy. But Mom and I both love you. You know that."

"Where *is* my mommy?" Will balanced his plane on his wrinkled palm. "I don't like that I don't get to see her. Do you make her stay away, Daddy?"

"No." He would if he had to, until she got help.

Patrick had only cried twice in his adult life before the divorce. On his wedding day as Lisa had floated down the aisle like pure light and again at 3:24 a.m. on the morning Will came into their lives. Since the day his son was rushed to the hospital to be treated for hypothermia, however, he'd choked down more tears than the lead drama queen on the worst soap opera.

"You're turning into a prune, buddy. Ready to get out?"

Will tried to answer, but a yawn stopped him. By the time he managed to close his mouth, Patrick had him wrapped in a towel, halfway to his room.

They read their regulation three books before bed, and Patrick said his own silent prayer that the question of keeping Lisa away from Will wouldn't come up again.

He tidied up around the house. A client, who'd given up pickpocketing to earn a living by working for people like Patrick who couldn't keep up with their own housework, came by twice a week to do the big stuff.

Patrick liked keeping Ned Montgomery off the streets, but he felt strangely embarrassed with the reformed convict knowing that Patrick hated to pick up newspapers after he read them. Or that Will had never managed to get a towel into a hamper.

After he ran out of mindless chores, he turned on one of the twenty-four-hour news channels. All the while, his thoughts drifted back to Daphne.

Was he a man or a barely surviving divorced father whose ex-wife had convinced him no one could change?

RAINA MET DAPHNE on the front porch. Her smile widened when Daphne got out of the loaner.

"You got a new car."

The little sedan was hardly new. It sported a dent in the front panel closest to Raina, and a scratch all the way from hood to taillight. A hailstorm had pocked the paint job with dings. But it looked better to Raina than Daphne's own car.

"I borrowed it from this guy named Kent while my car's in the shop. The radiator blew."

"I know Kent. He did some transmission work for my mother a couple of years ago."

"You like his work?"

"Sure." Raina snapped her fingers as if she remembered why she'd hurried out. "I did something today. I don't want you thinking I don't want you in the house."

Daphne thought she might cry. "Are you throwing me out?"

"Are you nuts?" Raina turned away from the front door. "Come this way. I know you haven't been comfortable, and you feel as if you're living off me."

"I don't mean to seem ungrateful, Raina."

"You don't, but I'm not comfortable with taking rent for a room."

She waved her hand and Daphne followed around the driveway where the small shrubs were fleshing out.

"Where are we going?"

"We're here." Raina pointed to the bank of four windows set into a brick addition that rose above the garage. "That's an apartment. About a billion years ago, my great-grandfather's housekeeper and butler lived up there with their children." She pulled a key from her pocket and started up the brick spiral staircase. "I'm afraid spiders and old luggage live there now, but we can clean it out for you."

"I can't take it." Daphne hung back. "That place may be servants' quarters to you, but it's nicer on the outside than any apartment I've ever rented."

"Well, I think it's more appropriate since you're insisting that I take your money."

"I can't afford this much, and I don't want to look at it. I love old places and I'll fall in love with it, I'm sure."

"It's not like the rest of my house, and you aren't going to pay me a thin dime more than you do."

"This might be better than your place." Daphne climbed slowly, certain she'd be a sucker for Victorian beams and molding, unblemished by fancy, twenty-first-century style.

"I was right." Raina had already opened the door and was wiping cobwebs off her face. "I should have had the place cleaned before I showed you."

But Daphne saw through the cobwebs and dust and stacks of detritus, to the bones and the bare wood and the thick, cool plaster. "If I moved in, you'd have to blast me out with a cannon."

Raina swung around. "You like it?"

"Like it?" Daphne flattened her hands on the pale wall, a little beige from dust and dirt. "It feels like home."

"I've never felt that way."

It took a few minutes for Raina's words to sink in. "What do you mean?" Daphne brushed dirt off of her skirt. "You've lived here all your life."

Raina took up a position behind two steamer trunks and a carriage lamp. "I know I'm the lucky one. I had a mother and father who loved me more than anything they ever owned, and they owned all this." Her hands, held wide, encompassed the apartment and the house, the grounds and probably half the town. "I never went hungry and I was never afraid, but I don't know who I am, Daphne. I don't even know who I want to be."

"I don't want you to be sad." Without thinking, she hugged her twin.

Raina stared into her eyes. "Have you realized

you and I won't ever need a mirror again? We can just look at each other."

"You're changing the subject." Daphne let her go, but she refused to back off from admitting she loved Raina. "I'm embarrassed because you can help me when I'm sort of homeless, and I can't promise you anything but thanks, which you don't want. That's who you are."

"Giving you rooms to live in and an old stove to cook on is easy. Telling you I don't want you to leave Honesty—that's hard. My father died so long ago I hardly remember his face. That scares me." She looked up, her own features drawn. "My mother— her death hurts me every day I wake up and remember that she's gone."

Tears burned away Daphne's rough day. She hugged her sister again. "I don't want to leave," she said. "You're not alone. You won't ever be alone again unless you ask me to go."

"We have something else in common." Raina squared the corners of the two trunks. "Neither of us is comfortable feeling needy."

"Needing each other feels okay." Daphne caught the trunks. "I came here because I thought if someone else loved me, I'd be safe. But you've done so much more for me. You've become my sister and now I feel protective. My heart doesn't seem to know the adoption agency split us up."

"I still don't see why they did that."

Daphne scoffed. "I don't care anymore. My life starts here and now."

Daphne meant what she said. She had dropped off her information with the attorneys in town. Some had seemed interested.

"I envy that. I wish I knew what I wanted to do."

"You must know your identity's all tied up with your mother. How long was she sick?"

Raina's tension tightened the air. "All my life in one way or another."

"What could you do but take care of her? What you're missing now is a job that you choose." Daphne leaned into the stuff behind her and something scraped across the floor. She straightened, alarmed at ruining Raina's property. "You may not have wanted your chance for a new start to happen this way, but that's what you have, and you should run with the one thing you most want to do."

Raina covered her face with her hands and then yanked them away. "First step here is to clean the place so you can live in it. You want it, don't you?"

"It's tempting, but I'm not paying you near enough."

Raina shook her head. "I don't need the money. Let me do the sisterly thing now and help you find a safe place to live." Raina crossed to the wall, rubbing the grime with a cloth. "I wonder if this will come clean, or are we going to have to paint? The plaster's in good shape."

"You want to start tonight?"

Raina finally turned. "I know you want to be with Patrick, but I'm kind of glad you're still here with me."

"I think I love him, Raina."

"I know."

"But he's afraid, and I deserve better." She grinned and hugged her sister again. "You made me see that. And you and I are always going to be together from now on. I was serious about that cannon."

A COUPLE OF NIGHTS LATER, Daphne found a Laundromat off one of the side streets north of the courthouse. Using the laundry in Raina's house felt presumptuous, though she knew her sister would call that ridiculous.

She dropped her Hefty bag in front of a machine that had probably started service around the time she was born.

Detergent. She found a vending machine and kept feeding it quarters until it finally accepted six. But then the detergent it traded didn't want to come out of the box.

Humidity had swollen the powder into a fat lump. This little box might have been in that machine for a decade or more. She had to tear the cardboard and then break up the bloated square.

"Your colors are going to run if you put everything in the same machine." A small woman leaned in at Daphne's elbow.

"I don't think I have enough to use two."

"We'll share."

"Oh." The woman was older, her hair gray, her eyes tired. Her closet might be as empty as Daphne's for the same lack of disposable income. "Okay."

"I have whites," the woman said. "You can put in anything light colored."

"Cool." She plucked out the softer colors, not wanting to dye her new compatriot's clothing.

"You look like someone I know," the woman said.

Raina got around. "I hear that a lot. Who?"

"You can't be her. She'd never set foot in a place like this."

"You might be surprised." Daphne couldn't let anyone bad-mouth her twin. "I'll get another box of soap if my quarters hold out."

"No need." The woman dragged a bottle of liquid detergent out of the wire basket she'd rolled behind her.

"I don't want to use yours."

"We're sharing."

"Thanks, I meant to say."

"Sure."

They loaded the machine and then sat together in companionable silence on plastic chairs that skidded a little under their weight.

Daphne ignored the stares of people who also seemed to think they recognized her. She spied a stack of magazines in another one of the rolling baskets the place provided and sifted through them until she found a gossip mag only eighteen months out of date.

"You want one?" she asked her new friend.

"Nah." The other woman waved her hand.

Daphne sat and leafed through the old news.

"What is your name?" the woman asked.

"Daphne Soder." She offered her hand. The woman shook it in a small, tight grip.

"I'm Clea Taylor."

"Hi, Clea."

"That lady you look like. She's nice enough."

Daphne closed the magazine. "Yeah?"

"Sure. She comes to this place I visit. They call it a senior center, but it's not really. We just go there for lunch when we don't have something at home. That lady helps cook and serve the meals."

"She cooks." She tried to imagine Raina in her white suit, peeling carrots or rolling out biscuits.

"I like when she's there. She doesn't act like she's doing us a favor. She asks about my granddaughter."

"That is nice. Sometimes those do-gooders just pretend they're listening." She offered a silent prayer that Raina would forgive her for calling her a name.

"She really does do good." The woman hesitated. "My grandchild is a boy, but she tries. No one else remembers I have anyone. Or at least they don't take the time to talk about it."

"I think I was supposed to meet you tonight, Clea."

"Huh?" She looked suspicious.

Daphne backed off. Once she'd been like her new friend, a person without anyone or anything to count on. Flippancy could frighten a woman like that.

"I mean I've enjoyed talking to you. I really have."

"Oh. Me, too." Clea's face reddened. She got to her feet slowly, as if her body ached. "I'm gonna check on our stuff."

Daphne tossed the magazine onto the chipped Formica table at the end of the seats. Funny, she'd been in Laundromats so many times and yet tonight she felt as if she didn't belong here.

The old antsy feeling started almost like a tickle in her stomach. She couldn't name it—depression or just plain uncertainty. Fueled by Patrick's real and possibly even sensible fears, it grew stronger, wrapping spindly arms around her chest until she couldn't breathe.

She wiped her mouth.

How good would a drink taste? At first, she'd been picky. Glenfiddich, thirty years old, had assuaged her shame. Then she'd learned to make do with twelve-year-old.

Finally, her discerning tastes had given way to expedience. Turned out you could break the steel arms with beer-on-sale just as efficiently. Hell, she'd fought the monster off one night with a particularly potent cough syrup. She stretched her legs out in front of her, staring at her worn sneakers.

Was she desperate for a drink or for another wrong man?

"We're on the spin cycle," Clea said, standing in front of their shared machine.

Daphne went to wait beside her. The cycle had just started, but standing so close to Clea, she realized how tiny her washing partner was. A nice fat sandwich wouldn't be amiss.

"Clea," Daphne said, "could you watch our things? I'm starving, and I'd love something to eat. Have you ever eaten at that sandwich place on the square?"

Clea looked as if she'd love to decline Daphne's offer and just as much love not to. She folded her hands together and pressed her fingertips against her lips.

"I really like tuna salad," Daphne said.

"They have the best I've ever tasted."

"Think you'd want some chips?"

"Have you ever had those sea-salt and vinegar ones they cook in a kettle?"

"I love those." She'd never heard of such things, but she'd find them.

As she walked out of the Laundromat, she glanced back. Every article of clothing she owned in the world was either in those machines or on her back.

Clea was still standing where she'd left her. Daphne put on a little speed. You had to choose to trust.

She was walking back to the Laundromat when Patrick's car passed her, moving slowly enough to let her see inside—even if she wished she could look away. He and Will were chatting. Neither saw her, and then suddenly, a little hand lifted in a wave.

She waved back, with the hand holding the sandwich bag.

She grinned. No matter what his parents' divorce had done to him, or how Patrick worried for Will, he remained a loving little guy.

As SOON AS her wash dried, Daphne folded her clothing and trotted it out to the loaner. Clea waved goodbye, pushing her basket of clothing and detergent, topped with the bag holding over half of the longest tuna salad on a roll Daphne had been able to buy from the sandwich shop.

"You sure you don't want a ride?" Daphne asked.

Clea shook her head with dignity. "I don't have far to go."

Honesty looked so pretty from the square and the shopping area around Miriam's shop, but Daphne wondered where Clea would be stowing her clean clothes that night.

She wove around the square until she found a parking spot near the church. As usual the side door stood open.

The nights continued to bring fear back to Daphne. Fear that she wasn't as strong as she believed.

The meeting helped, though she'd finally learned only she could find her resolve.

The church service must have ended at the same time as the meeting. Parishioners moseyed down the stairs, not always discernible from the group who'd met with Daphne.

Gloria Gannon stepped out of the crowd. "Daphne?"

"Hey."

"How are you?"

"Fine. How are those cookies coming along with Will?"

"We've made a few more. You should come help us eat some."

"I'm not sure Patrick would like that."

"You did tell him, then?"

"He knows."

"Does he know he's in love with you?"

Daphne's breath caught. She looked right and left, afraid of being overheard. "I don't know that."

"I think you might be fooling yourself. I know Patrick's fighting for his son." The other woman made her tone gentle. "But I care about mine."

"I don't want to be a problem for either of them."

"You can see why he'd be careful."

"I can't confess my sins on the village green and promise to sin no more."

"Patrick doesn't see you that way."

"I don't think you've really talked to Patrick about it." Daphne started for her car.

"I don't like to see you upset, either."

Daphne stopped and turned her head. Gloria looked anxious, a little sad. "Why?" Daphne asked. "You don't know me."

"You saved my grandson. You stopped that man, and yet you felt some sympathy for him. You're not a bad woman."

"Just bad for your son."

"I don't believe that. But if Patrick can't be sure you're safe for Will, he feels he has to stay away from you."

"So he sent his mother to explain." Daphne walked away, ashamed of her temper, and yet, nothing would have dragged her back.

CHAPTER TWELVE

"YOU DID WHAT?" Patrick shut the car door at the sheriff's office. Gloria had come to view a lineup and he'd come to support her.

"I like Daphne. I just wanted her to know she was welcome at my house no matter what you choose to do."

"You understand I'm trying to be a good father for Will?" She sent him a look and he shook his head. "How masculine do I look if you're out harvesting women for me?"

"I'm serious, Patrick. You're making a mistake because you were a little blind with Lisa. Lisa's in the past."

"I'm just wondering what more we can do to hurt Daphne. She ought to be able to walk out of a church without you matchmaking when she and I know where we stand."

"Neither one of you has a clue, and I blame you."

"You're probably right to, but don't bother Daphne anymore, Mother."

"She'll be in there."

"Maybe not." Pathetic. "They won't want the two of you to meet and discuss your selection."

"I shouldn't have spoken to her at the church," Gloria said, "but you need to. You hardly know the woman and yet you're hoping for a glimpse of her today."

"Mother—"

"Everything you feel for Will, I feel for you, and I hate seeing you unhappy. You're lonely."

"Not for Daphne."

Gloria wasn't about to let him off the hook. "Do you ever think about what you're going to do when Lisa comes back?"

"I rarely think about anything else. But right now we're going inside this building so that you can identify the guy who grabbed Will. Is now the best time to talk about Lisa, even if she didn't influence him?"

"I'm just saying, one way or another you'll have to learn to trust that a woman can beat addiction."

"Okay. Let's go inside."

At the reception area, an officer took her toward the back and invited Patrick to cool his heels. He'd hardly waited two minutes when the door from the back opened and Daphne came out.

Her face was tense. Tears pooled in her eyes.

Frowning, he went to her. "You didn't recognize him?" he asked.

"I did."

Around them, people milled like ants in a colony run amok. A woman screamed that her daughter was not guilty. A man described the wallet he'd lost in the parking lot of Draper's Diner.

Over all those voices, Patrick kept hearing Daphne's, half-broken by dismay. "I did."

"Do you know that guy?"

She shook her head, but something in her eyes frightened him. "You admitted he was the one? You identified him?"

"Yes, yes." She seemed to hear the rage, blowing up like a balloon to fill his head.

"But you didn't want to?"

"Of course I wanted to." She took his hand and pulled him out of the office, all the way to the street, where sun beat down on his skull and he could barely think. "I find it hard to take when someone like that guy—or me—gets so wasted that doing bad things becomes easy."

"Stop." Patrick put his arms around her. He cradled the nape of her neck and turned her face into his chest. "I don't want to hear you compare yourself to him."

"I don't have any sympathy except that I've been that desperate and the memory scares me." Her voice was muffled, but she wouldn't give in and give him peace.

"Patrick?"

He turned. Daphne sprang back as if Tom Drake, the sheriff who was watching them from the steps above, had thrown ice water on them.

"We need to talk," Tom said.

Patrick glanced at Daphne. She yanked at the hem of her blouse, smoothed her jeans over her thighs and walked away. Patrick scowled after her, but joined Tom.

"What's up?"

"Lisa's coming home. You need to prepare

yourself. She's in a rehab facility in California right now, but in a few months she'll be home. According to her attorney this thing with Frank was a wake-up call. She's going to seek a change in custody when she returns."

Patrick turned. Daphne was out of earshot. Even if he yelled her name, he doubted she'd come back.

THE WEEKS PASSED, turning spring into summer. Danny Frank, looking a little healthier and clean after six weeks of jail food and iron-bar-enforced abstinence from narcotics, pled guilty, and received a sentence of three years.

In the same six weeks, Daphne and Raina turned the apartment over the garage into a cozy nest where they spent most nights watching TV, talking, devouring popcorn and those kettle-cooked chips Clea had introduced Daphne to.

"I wish we could find her," Raina said one night over fajitas and a Johnny Depp marathon.

Daphne paused the movie. "She thought she'd seen you at a senior center."

"I just don't remember anyone who sounds like her. And I always ask about her granddaughter?"

"Who's actually her grandson."

"That's embarrassing." Raina cut a bite of fajita. Daphne made a face and lifted hers in her fingertips. "I'll look for her again in the fall," Raina continued. "Some people don't come in until it's cold."

"Maybe I could work there in the fall?"

"You want to?" Raina asked.

"Sure. It's about time I gave back to this community." Daphne grabbed a tortilla chip and soaked it in the queso they'd made. "It gave me you, and you've given me everything else."

"You're using family hand-me-downs." Raina peered around the polished, uncluttered family room, about twelve feet square, bound by a TV that presented in color but hadn't communicated with its remote in decades, and a set of three bookshelves that held all Daphne's treasures. "And you're probably the only person who's ever read anything in the library."

"You should grab a book now and then."

"I've been thinking about it. I'm going to nursing school."

"What?" Daphne sat straight up. "I'm impressed."

"Well, not nursing school exactly. White Rock College offers a B.S. in nursing and it's only a forty-five-minute drive. I've been working on my application."

"Like they'd think twice before scooping up an Abernathy." Daphne nibbled another chip and sank against the couch with a sigh of repletion. "You'll have no problem getting in."

"My great-grandfather did endow their school of pharmacology, but I'm not mentioning that in my app."

"Good idea. No need to whack anyone over the head with a wrecking ball."

"You sound like you think you're my mother."

"I think my soul's about five centuries older than yours and I see the world more clearly." Daphne rolled her head on the couch to grin at her sister. "So

I know you'll make one of the great nurses. I just feel bad for that old Florence Nightingale."

Raina stared at her and then laughed. "Her reputation's probably safe for a while."

"But this career will make you happy."

"Speaking of which, I hear they asked you to find a jury to put away Danny Frank. Before he pled-out, that is."

"Yeah. Prosecutors don't ask that often."

"You refused."

"No doubt sealing the deal with Patrick." She put her hand on her heart, otherwise ignoring its dull ache.

"Did he say anything?"

"Not a word. He got up and walked out, and I haven't seen him since. The guy's guilty, Raina. They were only willing to use me because they knew they could lose me as a credible witness because of my past and still have a great case because of Gloria."

"You're the one who looked him in the eye."

"I'm the known drunk. Gloria's respectable. And Patrick wants Danny buried because he thinks that'll make Will safe from Lisa."

"She's coming back."

Daphne slammed her feet from the coffee table to the floor. "Lisa? Is coming back here?"

"In a couple of months. She's in rehab. She wants Will back."

"Why didn't Patrick say anything?"

"He probably recognized it was already unethical asking you to help prosecute the guy."

"But I—" What? I love him. I want him to be safe, too? "I'm a coward. I should have taken the case."

"You're not a coward. The system will work. They were just hoping to stack the jury and the odds. Why did you say no?"

"So I could testify if it looked like he would get off."

Daphne hugged one of the cushions they'd sewn. "Is he all right?"

"Will?"

"I assume Will's all right or you'd have said. Is Patrick all right?"

"Why don't you ask him?"

A SOCCER BALL BOUNCED off Daphne's ankle, and her flip-flop flew into a green shrub.

"Aunt Raina, throw me my ball."

She used her finger to mark her place in *The Scarlet Letter* and picked up the ball. Will held out his arms like a basketball hoop.

"I'm Daphne," she said and tossed the ball. It went through his looped arms, garnering two points and Will's manly disdain.

"You throw like a girl."

"You're welcome." She leaned circumspectly into the shrub, trying to find her shoe and not impale herself.

The ball bounced off her backside.

"You can't catch, either, Aunt Daphne. You should come to my house and play because you need lessons."

She straightened, her shoe in one hand, the other stroking the offended area. "I rarely catch with that portion of my anatomy," she said. "You're not here alone?"

"My grandma's buying me candy. She said I could wait outside the shop." His little face wrinkled.

Daphne scanned the square. There was a confectioner's at the edge of the shopping area. He'd come a long way if he'd abandoned Gloria over there.

"Are you sure Grandma said you could wait outside?"

"Maybe she told me to wait beside her."

Holy crap. "Let's find your grandma. I'll bet she's worried if she's noticed you're gone."

"I saw you and I wanted to play."

Will cradled his ball in one arm and then slipped his other hand into hers. Daphne looked down at his tiny fingers, and tears startled her. She rubbed her arm across her eyes and looked for Gloria, who must be losing her mind.

"You know what, Will?"

"What?"

She pulled her phone off the clip on her purse. "Let's call your daddy." She paged back through her calls until she found the number for Patrick's office.

"Mr. Gannon is out," his assistant said.

"Could you reach him and have him call me at this number and tell him it's about his son? And that Will is all right." She gave her cell-phone number and hung up. "Have you seen Gloria yet?"

"Who's Gloria?"

"Grandma."

"Nope. Can we get a hot dog?"

"You don't scare easy, do you, Will?"

"You're not very scary." They walked a few steps. "But I don't want you on my soccer team."

"I don't blame you there," Daphne said. "But I do play better than that. You surprised me when I was reading and then I was looking for my shoe."

"You have to be ready at all times."

"You watch soccer on TV?"

He nodded.

"Good. I was hoping your coach didn't say stuff like that."

"Nah. He says you gotta have fun." Will's tone was disturbingly caustic.

"I like his way better."

"'Cause you're a girl."

Fortunately, her cell phone rang. She flipped it open and saw a local number. "Patrick?"

"You have him?"

"He was playing ball on the square."

"God."

"He's fine."

"We're walking away from the candy store right now," Patrick said. "Do you know where that is?"

"We're on our way. He's really all right except for being disgusted that I play soccer like a girl."

"You've been playing?"

She didn't blame him for sounding affronted. "No, which was my point when he insulted me. Here, I'll let you talk to him."

Will hung back when she held out her phone. "Is Daddy mad?"

"He's glad you're okay. Better talk to him." She reached for his ball.

"Hi, Daddy." Will peered up at Daphne, his eyes wide. "Yes, sir," he said. Then he shook his head. "I shouldn't have, Daddy. Is Grandma okay?" He waited a second. "Okay, but Aunt Daphne's a nice lady, too, Daddy. She helped me before and I knew she wasn't a stranger 'cause she has Aunt Raina's face."

Quick thinking. The little guy was smart. He handed her phone back.

"I think he's gonna be a little mad."

"Probably, because he's so relieved. You know, you shouldn't leave your grandma behind like that," she said.

"I know. That's what Daddy said." He grinned, all charm. "But I don't always wanna shop with Grandma, and I like hanging out with you."

Daphne smiled. At least one of the Gannon men didn't feel he was throwing away his chance at a clean future by talking to her.

"Daddy." Will shot down the sidewalk, dropping his ball to reach his father and grandmother, whose worried faces magically relaxed.

Daphne chased the ball into the street and dawdled between a truck and a VW bug, allowing Patrick time to talk to his son.

"Hey."

She turned around. Patrick stood alone. His smile touched off a seismic event in her heart, but she fought to control it. "He's okay."

"Thanks. We're going to talk about the meaning of 'wait' and 'beside me.'" He took the ball, sliding his hand over hers. As if he also couldn't be close without wanting to touch her.

"Good." She smiled even when she felt as if she might explode in a dozen pieces.

"He trusts you, apparently."

"So he said. I'm glad," she said, "but I tried to explain about staying with his grandmother."

"Thanks."

Any more thanks and she was liable to confuse gratitude for a break in his boundaries. "I should go."

He glanced down the sidewalk. His mother and Will were waiting, unabashedly watching. "I wish things could be different," Patrick said.

"They could. You just have to learn how to trust, even though that feels impossible." Something about her nest-building with Raina, her few sweet moments with Will, had restored her self-confidence.

"If I could decide to change, I would have been at your door weeks ago."

"I'm not sure I'm your problem. Or Lisa, either."

"I have to get out of my own way?" He nodded and held out his hand as if she needed help back onto the sidewalk.

She let him pull her, shameless in her need to feel the warmth of his palm, the pressure of his fingers, twining convulsively with hers.

Daphne stared at the muscle working in his jaw. His eyes, all heat and banked emotion, made her heart stand still.

Suddenly, he pulled her close. "Maybe it's already too late," he said.

She held on, wanting to be closer, reveling in the play of his muscles beneath her hands. She breathed in his spice-and-male scent.

"No," she said. "It's not too late, but I won't wait forever, and I won't play this game of getting close and pulling back."

"I've wanted to see you," he said, his tone ragged.

"I've been worried about you. Raina told me Lisa's coming back."

"Daddy, what are you doing?"

Patrick stepped back, but then turned her in front of him. She was unsurprised to find Gloria and Will only feet away.

"Thanking Daphne for bringing you back to us." Patrick pulled at his tie as if it were choking him.

"Hunh," Will said. He held out a cellophane bag. "Want some candy?"

"We were actually on our way to lunch." Gloria lifted the plastic bag from her grandson's hands. "Maybe you'd join us, Daphne. Patrick's coming."

"I can't." She looked around her for Raina's book and caught a glimpse of Patrick's relief. She must have left the book on the bench. "I was on my lunch hour and I have to go back to work."

"Awww," Will said. "I could teach you some soccer."

"Some other day, we'll ask Daphne ahead of time," Gloria said.

"Thanks," Daphne said. "I seem to have lost something. I need to go back, but it was nice seeing you. Next time, Will, let's meet under better circumstances."

Patrick had the guts to look regretful as she walked away.

"What's cirumstirrups, Dad?" Will asked.

AT FIRST, Patrick thought the woman in Cosmic Grounds was Daphne. She had on jeans and a T-shirt. Her dark brown hair was in a loose knot on top of her head, but she looked up as he came closer, and he saw her eyes.

Raina was beautiful, but life hadn't colored her gaze with mixed memories of sadness and warmth, regret and a kind of joy he couldn't ever remember feeling.

"Hey." She gestured to the piles of paper in front of her. "Sit down. Tell me why I'm perfect for White Rock's nursing program."

"You are?" He took the chair across from her. "Since when?"

"Since I decided I don't have to fill my mom's shoes. I need some of my own."

"And nursing is a fit?" He picked up the forms, all neatly filled in. "I can see that."

"After a few minutes to consider?"

"I was surprised. I thought you'd just slide into your mother's chairs on all the committees in town."

"Which you don't respect."

"What's the matter with you and your sister? Do you have to challenge every word I say? I'm not sensitive enough? I don't respect enough?"

"You're not very sensitive. Too busy protecting

yourself." Raina went on as if she hadn't just poked him with a figurative ice pick. "But you should respect the amount of charity work my mother did. She kept half this town in warm clothes every winter."

"Who'll do that if you don't?"

"Her committees." Raina picked up a pen and poised it over her legal notepad. "She trained them well, and they still feel her influence. They've told me so."

"She was a born organizer."

"In the best way." Raina looked up at him. "Daphne thinks you're not sensitive?"

"Did she tell you that?" He hated asking it. He hadn't been in high school for a good many years, and even then he'd had the good sense not to play the "Did she say she liked me?" game.

"Daphne doesn't mention you at all."

"That explains why you're so mad at me." He stood and kissed the top of her head. Whatever it cost, he knew she was always in his corner.

"If she asks, I'll tell her your heart got incinerated along with your marriage, but you seem so insensitive because you're afraid of how much you care."

He laughed. "I'd rather you didn't. You make me sound so manly I might whip out some yarn and start knitting socks."

"You'll have to take care of looking manly on your own." She turned, making her chair scrape on the black tile floor. "She's not a bad person, Patrick. She had a problem—has a problem—according to her, but she deals with it every day. She won't let her guard down."

His cell phone rang and he pulled it out of his

pocket, mostly to keep Raina from seeing his expression. Then he read his divorce lawyer's number off the phone's display, and felt as if he'd been punched.

"Mitch?"

"Bad news, Patrick. We need to meet."

"Lisa's finished rehab?"

"She's petitioned for a new court date. She wants to see Will, and her papers say she'll finish her treatment in less than seven weeks."

The floor fell out from under Patrick. "Is the date set?"

"Not yet, but we need to prepare a response now."

"If she's been successful, I can't keep her away from Will. He needs her, too." His heart breaking for his son, Patrick looked at his watch and mentally took stock of today's calendar. "I can't meet you until after six."

"Fine. I'll be in my office. I'll have a plan and a draft document for retaining as much control as we can. Plus, we can require drug testing. Maybe we'll even get supervised visitation. You give your okay and we'll be set."

Patrick hung up the cell phone. Raina looked anxious.

"She really is coming?"

"She really is."

"Did she go into rehab?"

"According to Mitch, she'll finish in about seven weeks, but what does that mean? She can walk out of there and have a new prescription before she gets on a plane."

"Rehab worked for Daphne."

His doubts were pounding him full force. "I can't trust anyone right now, Raina."

Raina set down her pen with deliberation. "Who's asking for your trust? First of all, you're a fool for throwing away my sister. Daphne's not like Lisa. I'm trying to suggest that maybe Lisa has become more like Daphne. She finally sees she has a problem and she's making sure it doesn't hurt anyone else."

Optimism was one thing, but he'd never put Raina down as someone who could believe in Santa and the Easter Bunny and pie in the sky all at one time. "You saw him in the hospital that day, Raina. You're his godmother. How can you trust Lisa with him again?"

"The courts won't just hand him over without making sure Lisa is capable of taking care of him. But if she is well, she deserves a second chance and Will deserves his mother."

"The courts. How well did they take care of Daphne?" Every time he thought of her, scared and alone the way Will had been, he wanted to hit something.

"You're a lawyer," Raina said.

"For the defense."

"You don't trust the courts, but you trust your clients." She picked up her pen again, dismissing him. "And yet, you let my sister believe you don't care about her because you won't give her a second chance."

"I care about Daphne," he said, anger raising his voice. He felt the heads turn around him. Raina actually smiled.

He walked to the counter, deep in thought. His

son, who couldn't sleep without a night-light, ran to Daphne without a second thought, and Raina had so much faith in Daphne's recovery from alcoholism that she actually seemed to believe Lisa could also turn her life around.

What the hell?

CHAPTER THIRTEEN

DAPHNE STOOD BACK to admire the sage paint on her bedroom wall. Blue had been too intense. Yellow had somehow depressed her. This pale, warm green felt just right.

Someone pounded on the front door and she jumped, flicking paint into her hair.

"Come in, Raina," she yelled without Abernathy decorum.

The door opened.

"I think this green works. They called it sage at the paint store. Makes me think of Thanksgiving turkey when I say it—I'm kind of hungry—and it's thick so it coats the roller and I'm a slob with it, but I feel all warm and cozy."

"Looks nice."

She turned so fast she slopped paint down the wall. "Patrick?"

"I'm the last person you should let in here," he said, "and you're the last I should run to."

He was wearing an overcoat. The day had been cooler, temperatures hinting of an early fall, instead of staying where they should in mid-August, but an overcoat?

"What's wrong with you?" Without waiting for an answer, she set down her roller and wiped her hands on the drop cloth. "Are you hurt? Why are you cold?"

She opened his coat. What she expected to find she couldn't say, but she rubbed his shoulders and his chest, shuddering as her fingers bumped over the hard bumps of his nipples.

He stood in front of her, dazed, allowing her to pat him down. But then, she slid her arms around his waist.

"What's wrong with you?" she asked.

He swept his arms around her, and he took her mouth as if he owned her.

A traitorous part of Daphne, a small essence she didn't recognize, wanted to be owned, yearned to be swept away with the passion she'd felt for this man since his eyes had first frozen the air in her direction.

She forgot her anger and frustration as she shushed the alarm bells warning her that Patrick was going to regret what came next.

She opened her mouth and tasted the heat of the first man she'd ever wanted simply because he existed, because something in him seemed to fit with all the jagged edges of the self she'd managed to salvage.

He shrugged out of his coat, never lifting his mouth from hers. But she remembered something was wrong.

"Are you sick?" she asked, hardly knowing her own faint voice.

"Because I want you?"

"Because of the coat. Are you cold? Do you have a fever?"

"Shh," he said. "Please." He caught her face

between his hands. His fingers searched her skin as if for warmth. His mouth traced every inch of her face. She couldn't hide the tears he found in her eyes.

She'd had no idea she could want a man with her cheekbones and her temples and the bridge of her nose, but her whole body seemed to ache with longing.

He lifted his head, but only long enough to stare at her before he kissed her again. "You know I care about you?"

After the briefest second, she nodded.

He pressed their foreheads together. His mouth brushed her nose. "How can you hesitate?"

"Because you keep telling me I'm not good enough."

"Oh, no. I get that I'm the one who should be proving myself," he said. He pulled her close and she felt his mouth in her hair. Then he straightened abruptly. "What's that?" He touched his lips.

"You have green paint on your mouth." She lifted the tail of her tank top and wiped it. His half smile faded. When she dropped her shirt, his hands were already there, tight beneath her ribs. He slid one palm up, between her breasts.

She exhaled in a gasp. Patrick caught her shirt and pulled it over her head. He stared at her lacy, white bra as if he were feasting on her.

"You look better than I've been dreaming," he said. "Can I…"

Her blood seemed to slow and surge through her veins with the beat of her heart. This was crazy. It was probably wrong.

"I want to see you," he said.

"No preliminaries?"

"Please don't try to be funny." He leaned down and closed his mouth over her nipple. Lace and tongue, an unbearable, unbelievable combination, but not quite enough, either.

Groaning, she unhooked her bra. Her breasts seemed to swell as the lace dropped to the ground. She hardly felt naked. She wanted him vulnerable, too.

He cupped her breasts, but she reached for his shirt managing a couple of buttons before he jerked the rest and dropped the shirt behind him. He took her hand and pulled her into him.

The slide of his bare flesh against hers was so familiar she might have been touching herself. But oh, this was better. This was heat and life…and delicious.

Her nipples bumped through the sparse hair on his chest. He caught her breasts and lifted them, rubbing his thumbs over her so gently she cried out.

Patrick covered her mouth with his. His hunger, fierce, trembling, anxious to please, swept all good sense from the room.

Before she had time to consider consequences, Daphne undid his belt and found the button at the top of his zipper. She was frustrated with her own jeans when his pants hit the floor and his arousal thrust against her.

"The bed," she said.

He turned, pulling her with him. As he bent to take her nipples in his mouth again, she managed to undo her jeans.

Patrick threw off the drop cloths, lay back on the bed and reached for her. She pushed her jeans and panties off and then yanked his boxers down his legs, sighing when she saw him.

He smiled in appreciation of her approval and reached for her hands to help her crawl over him. They both moaned as she covered him.

He pressed his palms against her back and pulled her breasts to his mouth, loving first one and then the other. She wanted him with her, tried to reach his chest, but he caught her hands behind her back. Again, his mouth moved over her breasts until her body screamed for him.

"What are you trying to forget?" she asked. She'd made so many mistakes before. Patrick might be the one she couldn't recover from.

"Forget?" He kissed her, trying to shut her up, she feared.

"Tell me," she said.

"I can barely speak." He finally let her go, and his big hands covered her thighs. "Slowly," he said. "Let me help." He rocked her against him. His eyes closed as if he couldn't bear her to see what she did to him, but his nipples were hard. Goose bumps ran across his chest and arms.

He opened his eyes and pushed his hand beneath her hair. He pulled her down, taking her mouth. His legs lifted behind her as if he was trying to regain control, but she liked pushing him. She held him inside, teasing, pulsing, until he groaned as if he was losing himself.

The sensations masked common sense and reality.

He lifted her, and only at the last second did self-pres-ervation take over.

"Wait," she said, practically on a moan. She strug-gled to find her feet. Patrick reached for her.

"Daphne, come back," he said.

She couldn't answer, but she found what she was looking for beneath the bathroom cabinet. A long time ago, she'd learned to take no chances. She came back and put the condom on him. He held her hands, moving them to give himself pleasure, which she also found good.

This time, when he pulled her body over his, she sank against his chest and almost laughed at his harsh breath against her temple.

He raised her by her forearms and looked so deeply into her eyes as he lifted his hips, she had to look away. She straightened, putting instinct in charge.

In the faux darkness, threaded with emotion and need, she wanted to ask why. The word wouldn't come. She'd needed Patrick for too long, and if this was the only way they could say the things that mattered so much...

He lifted her and let her down again. And again. Over and over until her toes were curling. Sweat beaded on his forehead. She leaned down to lick it off, rocking her pelvis over him.

He grunted her name and caught her hips, holding her where he wanted her. He swelled inside her, and it was almost too much. She felt as if she were flying apart, as if Patrick were her safe anchor in a whirling world.

He held her until she landed, until she could think again and hold him and remember that something had brought him to her place.

His breathing slowly returned to normal. Hers didn't because fear had replaced passion. She rolled off his chest and went to the bathroom.

Her face in the mirror startled her. Pink stained her cheeks. Her hair stood in a curly nightmare.

Her roused nipples and the reddish marks on her stomach and hip made her reach for the robe behind the door. She slipped it on. She was tying it with firm hands when Patrick appeared.

"What are you hiding?" she asked.

"That you make my life make sense, and still I can't have you." He pressed his mouth to her forehead and then stared at her in the mirror, the stranger with those icy eyes again. "Lisa asked for a court date."

"Lisa?" She barely remembered his ex-wife's name with lovemaking still flushing her body. "No court is going to give her Will."

"She's been in rehab." He walked back into the bedroom and picked up his boxers. "I guess someone will believe it's worked."

She watched him step into his underwear. "So you wanted to forget."

"No." He couldn't lie. He lifted his head, some guilt in his gaze. "I did, but it was more than that. I wanted to feel safe again. And I wanted to be with you. I wanted to make love to you and pretend everything would be okay."

"Pretend?" She tightened the belt on her robe. "Well, you did a great job. Now you should go."

"What?"

She handed him his pants. "Go. I don't need pretend."

"I'm telling you everything. I meant to tell you everything."

"After." She lifted his shirt with her toes and caught it in one hand. "This is yours, too. Take it and your lies and get out of my home."

"Lies?"

"I asked what was wrong. You said 'nothing.'"

"You could have talked then?"

"You didn't want talk from me. You wanted sex. Now you can find someone to talk, who'll make it all better."

"I want to talk to you, Daphne. I wanted to ask what made you change, how you know you won't drink again. Raina said I didn't care about you, but I do. I kept saying so, but you wouldn't believe me. Surely you know now."

"If you'd said something, that might matter." She turned away. "But you used me, and I let you. You're going to kill anything I feel for you."

"I know I'm not a good man right now, but I need your help."

"Bad news for you," she said, her heart shattering. "I don't know that I'll never drink again. And neither will Lisa. She can promise. She can cajole. She can bargain with the devil, but no one can make her stop her bad habits except herself. And the same goes for you."

"My bad habits?"

"Mistrust. Apparently, feeling so superior to me in your fine, sober state that you have no problem using me for sex, pumping me for info on how an addict lives, and then running back to your nice safe hidey-hole."

All the while, she'd been urging him through her three rooms, plus kitchen area. At the front door, he had his pants in one hand, his shirt and jacket in the other and an annoying, quizzical look on his face, as if he couldn't understand what made her so unforgiving.

"I expect respect from my friends—and my lovers." She reached around him to open the door, shoved him out and slammed it in his face.

AT THE BOTTOM of the stairs, with his shirt on and his pants finally buttoned, he ran into Raina.

His first thought was to plunge his head into the nearest pile of sand. His second was more to the point. Daphne needed someone. He'd hurt her badly.

Raina looked him up and down.

"What the hell have you done to my sister?"

"She threw me out." That part didn't matter as much as the pain that had made her hunch inside her robe. "Will you go up there?"

"I plan to as soon as I chase you to the car with a shotgun. Are you out of your mind?"

"I must be." How could he explain no one except Daphne would do when he was terrified for Will? No one else could make anything feel right. "I'll give you my father's shotgun if you'll just try to explain I needed—" It was difficult to say to Raina. "I needed to be with her. I didn't mean to use her. I'm frantic for my son, and I wanted to—"

Lose himself? Forget the fear of the moment when he'd have to put Will's hand in Lisa's? Neither were good reasons to make love to a woman who'd made him feel he was the only man who'd ever mattered to her.

"I'll tell her she's going to be okay despite you being a complete jerk, for God's sake. Get your clothes on straight and go home and make sure you can explain this to yourself before you set foot near Daphne again."

"If I could imagine how to have her and Will and not make any more mistakes, I'd be up there still."

"Instead you're running off, half-dressed. Why not tell *her* you care?"

"I tried, but she threw me out."

Daphne had seen straight through him and so did Raina.

She handed him the sock that had dropped at his feet. "I think you're wrong. You should give her a break, especially after what you've done. You have some nerve talking about what danger Daphne might bring your family. I'm positive you've damaged mine."

"Leave him alone, Raina."

They both looked up, startled to find Daphne on the landing, her hair in order, her face still glowing, but drained of emotion.

"Please let me come back up and try to explain," Patrick said.

"You need a good woman, an ordinary, never-been-in-jail, never-slept-under-a-bridge, Honesty kind of girl to keep Will safe. Then you'll feel safe, too. I'm not ever going to be her."

He climbed the stairs. "Go away, Raina," he said. She stayed at the bottom. "Give us a second of privacy."

At the top of the steps, he faced Daphne, but nodded toward her sister. "At least you got what you came here for," he said.

"Yeah, but I wanted more."

"You're not afraid to say that," he said.

"I don't have a son, and I'm not using him to make sure I don't get hurt."

"You're saying this is about me, not Will?"

She touched his cheek. "I don't ever want to see you again. I don't want to infringe on your friendship with Raina, but you and I are done."

"I'm sorry," he said. "I couldn't think straight. I should have talked to you right away."

"If you'd just said, 'My ex-wife is coming back to town. I feel a hole opening underneath me,' that would have worked. I'd have asked you in. I'd have done anything to make you feel better."

"I'm afraid if I let you into my life, even that much, I'll never—"

"Be able to get rid of me again." She stepped away. "Well, you took care of that. Goodbye, Patrick."

He wanted to beg her to rethink, to consider

what never seeing him again would be like, because he assumed it would be unbearable for both of them.

But he'd done enough and then some. She deserved a better man.

"Goodbye, Daphne."

He half expected to find Raina returning to the bottom of the stairs, but she'd gone back to the big house, or she'd simply walked out of sight. Shame sent him to his car without trying to explain.

Loving Will more than his own life couldn't excuse what he'd done.

THE FUNNY THING about Daphne's cleansing shower was that she hated washing Patrick's touch away. She'd been as desperate as he more than once. She'd done things simply to feel good for a moment, not letting herself consider the consequences of the moment after.

But, as with Danny Frank, she could feel empathy and yet be determined he wouldn't get away with it.

Drying her hair, she thought she heard a knock on the front door. She straightened and set the blow-dryer on the counter. "Coming."

She shut the door on her rumpled bedroom and hurried to the front of the apartment. Raina was on the landing.

"I bring commiseration." She lifted two long brown bags.

"I hope those are baguettes."

Raina shook her head. "Nope. Yours is sparkling grape juice. Mine is wine—the cheap kind I like instead of the good stuff my mother kept in the cellar."

"You don't want to go in the cellar because you remember her down there."

"I remember her everywhere."

"Suddenly, I realize I just can't help analyzing any unsuspecting soul who wanders past me. Possibly as a way to ignore my own problems." Daphne led the way to the kitchen. "But you shared wine tasting. That was something special you did together, so you mourn for that the way you mourn for her. Every time you go to the cellar."

"You're changing the subject," Raina said.

Daphne opened a cabinet and turned, brandishing two of her best bright blue plastic disposable cups. "Because I feel like an idiot."

"Why did you do it?"

"I love him, and I'm thinking love makes me stupid."

Raina took the cups and opened the sparkling grape juice first. "Is it all right for you to do this? Hang out with me while I drink wine? I can have juice with you."

"It's probably not a great idea to follow a drown-my-sorrows ritual, but I don't expect you never to drink again. Your wine is fine as long as I don't drink it." Daphne took her cup and went to the fat sofa Raina had remembered her grandmother using. "Are you upset because it was Patrick?"

"I'm pissed as hell," she said with un-Raina-like emphasis. "He ought to be glad I don't have a shotgun."

"I'm not entirely comfortable talking to you about him."

"I told you a long time ago. He's my best friend. Nothing more, and not much of that right now."

Daphne couldn't forget Patrick's desperation. He had needed her. Or he'd needed a body that attracted him.

That idea wouldn't leave her alone. "Would he have found a friendly hometown girl if I hadn't been so damn available?"

"I look just like you. If he was going after a type, he'd have noticed I'm a woman before now."

"He notices women." No man who made love like that could not notice. He knew how to please, damn him.

"He was angry with me because I said he didn't care for you. Did you think he loved you?"

Did she? Of course she did. And the thought that she'd been wrong hurt. "Raina, do we have to talk about it? I know I made a massive mistake, and I won't repeat it."

Raina brought her glass over. She sat on the couch, curling her feet beneath her. "He's like a brother I take for granted. I do love him, and I worry that he'll never trust anyone again because of Lisa." She drank and then rolled her head on the back of the couch. "I don't want him to overprotect Will so much he'll be afraid, too."

"You don't have to worry about that. Will acts first and thinks later. If anything, I'm on Patrick's side where Will's concerned. I nearly coughed up a lung that day he hit me with his ball because he'd wandered off again."

Raina sat back. "Why? Has Patrick infected you with his suspicious nature?"

"Maybe Patrick and I believe the worst can happen because we've seen it. What are you thinking that has your forehead tied in knots?"

"That maybe you and Patrick aren't as impossible together as I thought. That kid needs breathing space."

"He's five years old."

Raina sipped her wine. "Patrick should get over it all so that Will can."

"Get over it? Will's his child. Imagine losing a child because a woman you loved cannot and will not take care of him. Because right now she loves drugs more."

"I'm sorry for that, and you can count me among the adults who'd protect Will with their last breaths. I'm grateful Lisa's never managed to get her hands on him, and I hope she'll have to jump through hoops to be his mother again, but you're my family, and I don't want to lose you."

Daphne sat back, surprised that Raina couldn't see how much she loved her. "You nut. I'm not going anywhere. Even though I'm going to feel a little shame for being so stupid every time I see that man."

"For caring too much, you mean. Listen to me. Forget I'm the sheltered little girl you saw in that chair in Patrick's office. You don't have the corner on human behavior. Patrick thinks you can't stop drinking, but he couldn't control a couple of his basic instincts tonight, either. And no matter what you say, I am afraid you'll go away again. What if you decided you couldn't live in town and look Patrick in the eye?"

Her voice broke. Daphne stared, her throat tight. "What's in this grape juice?" She held up her fine plastic stemware. "I feel like crying."

Raina stared at her, both eyebrows lifted.

"Sorry," Daphne said. "I meant I love you, too. I thought you'd be on his side if we ever came to this."

"You're my sister." She set her glass down. "Not that I want either of you to make me choose."

Daphne pulled her own feet up underneath her, smiling because she realized she and Raina probably looked like bookends. "I'm glad you didn't take sides the moment you saw us tonight."

"I sort of did. I told my best friend to stay away from my sister until he could explain himself. And I want a damn good explanation."

"That's a reasonable stance, Raina. Not one that works in emotional situations, I fear."

"He didn't embrace it as great advice, either." Raina grabbed a pillow and punched it into the chair beneath her other arm. "Do you love him?"

Daphne ducked a straight answer. "He goes out of his way to help people. I'm seduced by that. He came to me the first night, when I was staying in the hotel, and he tried to talk me into moving. He didn't know me, but he wanted me to be safe."

"He does think he knows best about everything."

"Raina, he's still your friend. Don't assume he's

in the wrong." She had a sip of grape juice so sweet it made her grimace. "I didn't forget where the door was after I let him in."

"He knows he's not ready for a relationship right now. Coming here was selfish."

"He loves Will so much he's pretty much given up his own life. I've never known a parent like that. I may hate the way he thinks of me, and I won't see him again, but he believes it's all for Will. Until he figures out he's the problem, there's no way to fix it."

Raina went back to refill her cup. "I'm not sure he wants to fix it. No matter how much he wants you, he doesn't want to get hurt again, either. He really loved Lisa, too."

"So he's capable of love."

"I didn't say that to hurt you."

"I was serious. He knows how to love. We're just not right for each other."

"You are fine. Don't let Patrick persuade you—"

"Patrick's already in my past."

"I doubt it," Raina said, "and I'm supposed to the be naive one."

"I can't help wondering what's going to happen with Lisa."

"She's Patrick's problem. Yours is getting over him."

"That would be fine, except I can't stop loving him just because I want to, any more than he can stop holding back."

Raina had no snappy answer for that. But she sat next to Daphne, tugging her close.

"I don't know how you stop, but my shoulder's here for you."

"Maybe I'll just lean on you then. Leaning is so much nicer than crying like a kid."

"Yeah, that wouldn't help." Raina wiped a tear off her own cheek and they laughed.

HE'D RARELY DONE anything more idiotic. He hadn't meant to use Daphne. He wanted to call her, but when he reached for his phone, he couldn't find it.

His mother came out of the family room.

"You look horrible," she said.

He barely restrained himself from looking to see if his shirttail was wedged into his zipper.

"Try not to worry so much about Lisa. The courts have been on Will's side, and they'll continue to test her, so she won't be able to claim she's better without proof."

She patted his back. He didn't tell her the number of his clients who'd beaten drug tests.

"I'm fine. Thanks for staying. Did Will go to sleep easily?"

"I think he's in better shape than you."

"I hope he stays that way when his mother gets a court date."

"He will be better off having a relationship with her as long as the court keeps an eye on her drug use."

He could too-easily imagine himself going to pick Will up after a visit, finding Lisa, all her possessions and his son missing.

"I hope you're right."

"Call me if you need me, son." She took her purse from the bench and dug out her keys. "I'm a short drive away."

"Night, Mom."

As he shut the door behind her, he searched his pockets again for his phone. Not in his jacket or his pants. He must have left it in the car.

Anyway, what could he have said to Daphne to make anything better? He wouldn't lie to her and he couldn't tell her he saw their problem differently.

She fully intended to live sober every day of the rest of her life. He believed in her. But she also attended a daily meeting to remind herself not to give in to an overwhelming compulsion.

And the image that stayed in his head was of his son, on a gurney in the E.R., barely moving, calling for his mom who'd left him to nearly die.

Why did Daphne keep saying this was about him? Didn't she realize he had to keep Will safe?

CHAPTER FOURTEEN

"I NEED TO GO to bed." Raina stood, her feet unsteady. "How many glasses did I drink?"

"I'm not sure. Want me to walk you to the house?"

"No." Raina wrapped herself in the grape-soaked remains of her genteel dignity. "Don't mind me if you find me stringing a homemade alarm across the stairs."

"Alarm?" Daphne asked.

"Tin cans or something to warn you and me if Patrick comes back."

"I don't see him loading Will into the car so he can sneak back here in the dead of night for a hook-up."

Raina grinned. "I thought better of him, too, until tonight." She hugged Daphne loosely. "Will you be able to sleep?"

"After I paint a little." Assuming the paint hadn't hardened into glue. "Oh, man, I left the can open all this time."

"Paint, we can replace."

Daphne walked her sister down the stairs and pointed her toward the house's kitchen door. Back in her apartment she tossed their cups into the recycling bin and washed up.

At the end of the counter, she came upon Raina's open bottle of wine. It stopped her like a coiled, hissing snake.

She licked her lips, but dropped the sponge and put her hands behind her back.

One little sip. One small taste to cleanse her palate of the horrible, heart-stabbing day.

No one would ever know. Not Raina or her group at the church. Not Patrick.

She moved closer. Her mouth watered. Her cheeks almost hurt as she thought she could taste the wine's strong, dry bite.

No one had to know. She wasn't about to step into a car. She'd hurt no one.

Except herself. She'd break all the promises she'd made, and she'd become the woman Patrick feared most. More important, damn it, she didn't need wine. She needed to put her paint away and burn her sheets and go to bed.

With a nice sensible to-do list, she set to work.

SATURDAY MORNING, bright and early, she woke and sat up to find Patrick's coat on the floor near her door.

Raina could return that to its owner.

Just then, the pocket rang. She stared at it, tempted to answer, but too annoyed to help Patrick out. No doubt he'd discovered the phone missing.

She was tempted to walk on those pockets.

In a while she'd call and let him know it was still here. Until then… She picked up the coat, her only thought to toss it into Raina's yard.

Instead, she lifted it to her face. How sad must he have been to put on a coat in this weather?

The navy material smelled of Patrick, man and leather from his car and everything nice.

Tears caught at her with sharp claws. She resisted crying and threw the coat on the end of the counter.

Instead of hurling Patrick's goods into the great outdoors, she'd go out herself. Raina had said she could plant a small garden behind the garage.

Better to anticipate beautiful crocuses and tulips next spring than whiskey and a man she couldn't trust.

She'd already dug up the bed and prepared the soil. So she put on jeans and a T-shirt and drove into town to buy bulbs.

AFTER HE'D SEARCHED his car and his office and Mitch Espy's parking lot, Patrick finally realized he'd left his coat and his phone at Daphne's.

For a second, he considered asking Raina to pick it up, but she'd call him a selection of well-deserved names and tell him to get it himself. Again, he dropped Will off at his mother's.

"Where are you going?" she asked as Will ran to the kitchen to set out Play-Doh makings.

"I have to get my phone, Mother. I left it at Daphne's yesterday."

"What's wrong with you, Patrick? I think you're frozen inside."

"Why does everyone keep saying something's

wrong with me? I'm handling a problem that might cause pain for my son."

"And for you?"

"I'm attracted to Daphne. Mother, this isn't a conversation you and I need to have."

"I've been young. I've even loved the wrong guy once in a while—before I met your father, of course. I know how the world works."

"I'm the bad guy. Daphne did nothing wrong."

"You left your phone on purpose?"

When he thought about it honestly, he couldn't say his unconscious wasn't smarter than he was. "I'll be right back. I promise."

"You need to leave that young woman alone. She cares about you."

"I know. You're right."

"I saw her after an AA meeting."

"You knew, too?" he asked.

"She wanted to tell you herself. I thought that was brave."

"I meant I was trying not to mention it to you until you had to know. I never wanted to hurt her."

"What did you do?"

"All the worst things you can imagine. I can't defend myself, and I'll be lucky if she hasn't set my coat on fire. I'll be back. Okay?"

She followed him down the hall. "I'm not happy with you."

"Neither am I."

"Okay, then, but don't hurt that girl again just to scare her off."

He stared after her as she went to join Will. What did she mean about scaring Daphne off?

He'd been worried about women. He'd managed to alienate every one who meant anything to him. Daphne. Raina. His mother.

He drove, squinting at the sun, to Daphne's place. He half hoped she'd be gone, and then a second later, he swore at the thought of not seeing her again.

He parked in front of the garage. Her car was there. He searched for the ruins of his coat. It wasn't outside. He ran up the stairs to her apartment and knocked, but no one answered.

He leaned over the rail, searching Daphne's yard. "Hello?"

He froze. And then looked straight down.

"Daphne."

"You're looking for your coat?"

"It is here?"

"The pocket rang earlier."

"Why didn't you answer it?"

She peeled off gardening gloves and peered at him as if his brain might have stopped functioning.

"Ah," he said. "Dumb question."

"I'll come open the door."

"You lock it?"

"It's Raina's house." She climbed the stairs, digging the key from her back pocket. Those faded jeans were his favorites.

She opened the door and stood aside for him to pass. He saw the coat the second he was in. She'd hung it across the kitchen counter. He went straight to it and saw an open wine bottle.

He swore.

"What?" she asked. But when she reached his side, she knew. "Oh."

"Oh? That's all you have to say?"

Images flashed in front of him. Lisa, asleep with her head on the table when he got home from work. Will on that damn gurney, too tired to breathe.

And Daphne, assuring him she wasn't that kind of woman. He could trust her. She didn't want another drink. She'd never hurt his son.

His temper went for the roof. "I've felt guilty for—"

"This is your moment of truth," she said.

"Like that was yours?" He pointed at the beautiful bottle of glinting liquid.

"You have a choice."

He stared at her. "To join you in a glass?"

She breathed out as if he'd hit her.

"I'm sorry," he said. "I'm sorry, Daphne." He couldn't see her lifting that bottle to her lips.

"Don't let me off the hook. Think about this. I trusted you yesterday and you used me. I care about you so much I made love to you even though I knew something was wrong. What would make me drink?"

Suddenly, he couldn't make himself ask if she had. Asking would be beyond the pale.

"Can you be sure? If I tell you I didn't, will you believe me?"

He stared into her eyes, searching her, looking for the truth in her soul.

"You're afraid," she said. "But you have to ask. And then you have to choose whether to believe me or not. And you'll be choosing the way you'll believe for the rest of your life, because this is your only chance."

"Daphne—"

"And I love you," she said.

Joy slammed through his body the way they talked about it in books or movies. She loved him.

"But you're going to lose me," she said, "because you're afraid of being hurt. Not Will. You."

Silence ricocheted in that room like a heartbeat. He wanted to tell her she was wrong. He wanted to explain he was a man and he could handle his own problems, but he hadn't handled a damn thing. He'd reacted, from the day Will had almost died.

He'd been afraid to feel again.

He gasped because the truth was a blow as dangerous to Will, and to Daphne and to him, as anything she could do with wine.

He simply had to believe. He had to choose to believe.

"Stop." He held out his hand. "You don't have to say any more. I've been doing the same thing you did to hide. You drank to forget you weren't safe. You wanted to believe you wouldn't hurt anyone."

She stared at him. Yesterday lay in the shadow of her eyes.

"I've been pushing you away because I don't trust myself. I'm the one who brought danger to Will. I didn't see what Lisa was doing. I don't even know if I closed my eyes because I was busy, but Will was in danger because of me, as much as her, and I had to protect him. I had to find a way to keep him safe every day of his life."

"You can't do that," she said.

"Not if I want him to actually live." He took her hand, but he didn't dare ask her to come closer. "I believe in you, in the promises you make and the love you feel and the joy you've brought me."

"I love you, Patrick." She flattened her hand on his chest. "Will and I can learn to love each other, too."

"He's halfway there. And my mother would probably rather you were her child."

"You know I can't say I won't ever drink again. All I can promise is that I'll never do one thing near Will that could cause him a second's discomfort." She actually smiled, and his heart banged to get out of his chest. "Except I do indeed throw like a girl."

"You don't have to say that again." He kissed her. Thank God she kissed him back, with a fierceness he couldn't believe he deserved.

"Daphne." Her name was a pleasure. "I think about you all day long, and I can't sleep at night for wanting you.

"We had that physical thing down from the start. It was learning to trust." She hugged him tight. "In the face of wine bottles and fear."

No amount of fear was worth losing her. "I do love you."

"But?" she asked.

"No but." He pulled her arms around him. "Everything else comes after I love you."

"We have to be realistic. I could drink again. I need you to know that."

"If it happens, we'll work through it. As long as you want to stay sober, we'll manage. That's marriage, I guess," he said, not realizing he'd said it out loud.

Daphne froze. "Marriage? We'd better be sure we can make this work first."

He kissed her. "That should have hurt, you turning me down."

"Did it?" She traced the line of his jaw. Her warm, soft, seeking mouth raised his body temperature about a thousand degrees.

"I want you to know I'm not changing my mind because we had sex. I'm making a commitment."

"What did change your mind, Patrick?"

"Well, every woman I care about has mentioned I have a problem. And when you said this was my moment of truth, I knew I could stop hurting you if I just trusted you. Neither one of us could have stood much more. Maybe you've been giving me reasons to believe ever since I met you."

"Patrick." She wrapped her arms around his neck.

"Hmm?" He lifted her, and her legs went around his waist. Her breasts and thighs flattened against him, an invitation that ensured coherent thought would soon be impossible.

"Do you want to know about that bottle?"

"No." He opened her mouth with his and took her

back from the darkness of their doubts. She kissed him with generosity and love and forgiveness.

She leaned her head back. "Why don't we see just how sure you are that we're right together?"

"I'm damn near dying to show you."

EPILOGUE

"I THOUGHT YOU SAID your car was in the shop," Daphne said as her sister climbed into her passenger seat in the college parking lot.

"It is. The alternator or the ignition—I don't know what, but it's broken," Raina said.

"Isn't that your car, right over there?" She pointed at a white Mercedes three spots down and one row over.

"No. Are you kidding?" Raina shoved her bag onto the floor. "Let's go. I don't want my Spanish professor to see me."

"Why?"

"I—I don't like her."

"That's not like you." But Daphne put the car in gear and turned toward the end of the parking lot. "I still have to get candy, and I'm not sure Patrick will get home in time to put up the spiderwebs before the kids show up."

"I told you guys to do that last week."

"I know, but Patrick needed some help researching a case, and I owed an attorney in D.C. a prospective juror questionnaire."

"Patrick doesn't have a clerk?" Raina leaned

forward as they reached the main road. "I'm glad we're out of there."

"What's with you and the Spanish teacher?"

"Huh?"

"The one you don't like."

"She says I speak Spanish with a French accent."

"Why didn't you test through French?"

"I wanted to learn something new, Daphne."

"You're a funny woman. Can we stop at the grocery store?"

"Sure. I might stay and help you pass out candy."

"Will you?" Daphne turned into the street. "Good. Let's make Patrick hand out candy. When was the last time you trick-or-treated?"

Her sister didn't answer. Daphne glanced at her.

"You're kidding. Never?"

"My parents threw a party instead."

"Oh, sister, your life changes tonight. Will's convinced I'll let him go to more houses, so he and I have been campaigning to have Patrick stay home."

"Cool." Raina checked her watch. "I thought Lisa was coming for Halloween."

"She couldn't get time off from her new job." Lisa had decided California living suited her better after finishing rehab. "She's coming for Thanksgiving instead. Why do you keep looking at your watch?"

"Lots of homework and no time. Let's call Patrick and have him pick up candy. Or Gloria. She'll bring back the good stuff."

Daphne took a good look at the darkening sky. The tall pines rose around the interstate. They faced a few miles and probably some traffic getting into town. She'd hate to miss her first real Halloween with Will. Last year, they'd been so new to each other that she'd simply held his bag between houses and smiled politely at his haul. This year they'd mapped out the streets they wanted to visit. "That's a good idea. It's going to be dark by the time we get home. Will you call?"

Raina dialed Gloria. "Yeah, it's Raina. You're coming to Patrick and Daphne's for trick or treating?" She nodded at whatever Gloria said. "We were wondering if you could get the candy." After a few seconds, she looked at Daphne. "She's shocked you've waited till the last minute."

"I had some," Daphne whispered, "but Patrick and Will got into it during the World Series."

Gloria agreed and when they reached home, Raina suggested they turn into the street behind the town house to park.

"Honestly, this'll be better," Raina said. "People cruise up and down to get to the front doors on the other street."

"You're acting weird, and it's creepy going through the alley from here. Let's jump over the garden fence."

"Okay," Raina said. "I think we can do that."

They went into the kitchen door and found Patrick bagging the candy with his mother. He looked at Raina first. "You made it. Could you go check Will's costume?"

"Let me," Daphne said.

"No, Raina will do it. I really need some help here."

"Lots of help," Gloria said. "Because you two waited till the last minute. I won't tell you what I had to do to get this."

"If you're arrested, you're in good legal hands," Patrick said. "Come on, Daphne. I have to go check the spiderwebs out front."

"Did you finish?"

"The wind kept grabbing them. I want to make sure everything's okay."

He stopped at her side. With one hand, he stroked her cheek. "And I'm glad to see you. Did you have a long drive from the college?"

"I swear I saw Raina's car. Why would she lie about needing a ride?"

He kissed her without answering, and by the time he lifted his head, she didn't care. Looking at him, she forgot his mother. "Halloween gets to you."

"You do," he said. "Okay, Mom, I'm going. Sorry for embarrassing you."

He also disappeared.

"Like I've never kissed a guy. That son of mine assumes too much." Gloria stepped down the counter and showed Daphne the piles of candy. "One of each, the whole stack into one of these bags and twist on a tie and we're good to go."

"Okay." But she wondered how Will was doing with his werewolf costume.

"I have to—find a bowl." Gloria ran from the kitchen. "I'll check the sideboard in the living room."

Nice. Her first family Halloween and she was stuck alone in the candy assembly line.

"Grandma?"

Daphne turned toward the door, expecting to see a walking pile of hair, but she caught a glimpse of black and white before a hand snatched Will out of sight.

"Will?"

"I'm okay," he said.

"Come show me your costume. Where's the hair, buddy?"

"I'm—I'm not through yet."

"How are those candies coming?" Raina asked from the next room. "I'm looking for a bowl. Gloria went upstairs to see if she could find one."

"Upstairs? We have bowls in every cupboard. What's Will wearing?"

"That hairy thing."

Why should Raina sound confused?

The house went quiet again except for an occasional thump and then the front door opened and shut.

"Patrick? How are the spiderwebs?"

"Come look."

"I'll bring the candy." She filled a wooden salad bowl with a stack of the bags and hurried down the narrow hall. "Patrick?"

Music started, but it wasn't scary Halloween music. "This family has no clue about Halloween," she said, opening the front door. "You've got the wrong CD on. That's the wedding—"

She saw flowers instead of spiderwebs, Will in a tux and Raina holding a beautiful, white satin gown.

"Patrick?"

He looked even better than Will in his tux. It

hugged his broad shoulders and reminded her how tall he was. His eyes were nervous.

"This seemed like a good idea," he said, "but I'm thinking I should have asked you first."

"No."

"No?" he asked to a chorus of gasps.

"I'm glad you surprised me."

In his tux, he knelt on the flower-strewn porch and took her hand. Behind him, Miriam and Gloria and Raina and Will all cheered.

"Will you marry me?" Patrick asked. He glanced at the others over his shoulder. "Will you belong to all of us?"

She couldn't speak. She managed to fall to her knees and hold him, trembling. He turned his head against hers.

"Is that yes?"

She nodded, and he kissed the parts of her face he could reach. Over his shoulder, Gloria produced a prayer book from behind her back.

"I borrowed this from Reverend Brown."

"What for?" Daphne asked, and this time her nearest and dearest laughed as one.

"I'm marrying you," Gloria said.

Daphne turned to Patrick. "I'd rather we were legal."

"Absolutely." Gloria said. "I got my license over the Internet just for tonight. Get dressed, young lady. I want you good and married before the first ghouls arrive."

"I made sure," Patrick said as an aside.

As Daphne nodded, bewildered, Raina brought

the dress. "I hope you like it. It seemed right." She draped it over her arms, from beaded bodice to long narrow skirt.

"It's perfect."

They climbed the stairs together and Daphne dressed. Raina swept Daphne's hair into a loose bun that she held in place with a jeweled clip.

"Something borrowed," she said with a hug. "Are you sure?"

"Positive. He and Will are everything to me." She hugged Raina tight. "Along with you. You know that."

"You're going to be blissful."

She ran down the stairs ahead of Daphne. Patrick was waiting at the bottom.

"It's bad luck to see the bride before the wedding," Daphne said. "And we're going to have a Halloween anniversary."

"This is one of the luckiest days of my life," he said. "But you haven't had time to think about it. Do you want more time?"

"I can't wait, Patrick." She looped her arms around him. He held her with shaking hands.

"You make me forget how to think." He kissed her cheek and her chin and the lines of her collarbone, bared by the dress. "The honeymoon," he said. "Just tell me where, and I'll arrange it."

"Sometime, when Will is used to all this, we could do something special." She pressed her lips to his jaw. "But for now, could we rent one of those cabins on the lake? We could take Will with us. That would be wonderful."

"Perfect," Patrick said.

"Daddy, Grandma says it's time." Will came to them, dragging his feet. "Now I don't get this. Are we really getting married tonight?" He tugged at his collar. "I don't like this costume."

"We're getting married." Daphne knelt beside him. "Do you like the idea?"

"Sure." He hugged her tight and she saw stars. "I love you, Daphne, but can I put on my werewolf costume when we're done getting married?"

Laughing, she lifted him, and Patrick took him from her arms. "I say we all go trick-or-treating after we're married," Patrick said. "I want everyone in Honesty to see my family."

"I want some candy." Will patted Daphne's shoulder. "But since you're going to be my second mommy at last, I'll probably share some of it with you."

"Probably." Patrick kissed Daphne, briefly but well. "And how lucky are you, that he's my best wedding present?"

She didn't have to answer. She just laughed and they hugged each other, all three. Together tonight. Together for always.

* * * * *

A Fortune Wedding
by
Kristin Hardy

Red Rock, Texas
July 1991

"Come on, boy, come on," Roberto Mendoza muttered, crouching over the withers of Cisco, his big bay gelding, as they raced up the tree-studded grassy slope. The speed was intoxicating. The wind rushed over his skin. A kaleidoscope of sound filled his ears—the thud of hoofbeats, the rush of his own breath.

The silvery sound of laughter ahead of him.

And then they burst up onto the hilltop, the great blue bowl of the sky arching overhead.

"Hah! We beat you!" Frannie Fortune whooped, reining in her little chestnut mare and wheeling around. "Who says the girls can't outdo the boys?" With her short, sunbeam-blond hair and tilted eyes, she looked like a pixie, ready for mischief.

Life, Roberto thought, just didn't get any better than this.

"You girls only won because you took a shortcut," he told her.

"Don't blame us because we're smarter. We just took a faster way."

"Yeah, like straight up the side of the hill."

"Admit it, you're impressed."

He grinned. "I am, but next time you decide to take your shortcut, leave me with a suicide note for your uncle. I'm supposed to be watching out for you."

Her cheeks were still flushed with the excitement of the race. "I keep telling Uncle Ryan I don't need looking after. So I got thrown once. It can happen to anyone. You try staying in the saddle when a killdeer flies up between the feet of that monster you're on," she challenged. "See how you feel when your fanny hits the ground."

Roberto's lips twitched as he slid off Cisco. "I guess you'll have to come to my rescue."

"If you're lucky." She gave him an arch look.

How had he ever thought her standoffish? It hadn't been that, but simple shyness that had kept her quiet and to herself when she'd first arrived at the Double Crown Ranch where he worked. As the weeks had passed, she'd blossomed, quiet diffidence giving way to a sly humor that perpetually hovered around that delicate mouth, the surprisingly bawdy laughter that burst out of her more and more often as the days went by.

Maybe it was just being here, out on the ranch, amid the rolling terrain of Texas hill country. It could make anybody happy, although he might be biased. No matter where his life took him, Roberto thought, no place would ever feel as right as this patch of territory where he knew nearly every tree, bush and bird by name. It was in his blood, as much a part of him as his brown eyes.

Frannie walked over to stand next to him. "You think you'll ever leave here?" she asked, as if she knew what he'd been thinking.

He watched as she bent down to pick a long stalk of grass. "I'd have to have a real good reason. I figure I'll save my money, buy a place of my own someday."

Living and working out on the land, he couldn't imagine anything better. Certainly not sitting all day in a college classroom, no matter how much his father wanted him to. José Mendoza hadn't taken the news of his twenty-year-old son dropping out well. To avoid skull fractures from the two of them butting heads in the family's restaurant, Red, Roberto had come to work at the Double Crown, where his uncle Ruben Mendoza ran operations for the Fortune family.

And where the lovely, coltish Frannie had appeared for a visit just days later.

Too bad she'd somehow gotten snowed into dating Lloyd Fredericks, the original self-important, silver-spoon guy. But she was a Fortune and he was a Fredericks, so maybe they did belong together. It still set Roberto's teeth on edge every time he saw Fredericks drive in to pick her up. The jerk didn't deserve a woman like Frannie.

"So, what are you going to call your ranch?" Frannie interrupted his thoughts. "The Rocking RM? The Double R?"

"I was thinking Red Oaks."

"How about the Slowpoke?" she offered.

His eyes narrowed. "Remind me again who won when we raced last week?"

"That's because you had an unfair advantage," she argued. "Cisco's two hands taller than Peaches. We had to outsmart you."

What she'd done was about stop his heart when he'd seen her tearing up the side of the hill. She might have started out quiet and shy, but she was fearless now.

"You just got lucky this time," he said.

"No, I was prepared," Frannie corrected him, twirling her grass. "Lloyd says that's what luck is, just opportunity meeting preparation."

"That sounds like your boyfriend. Always looking for an angle."

She rolled her eyes. "He's not my boyfriend. We're just going out. Anyway, I don't want to talk about Lloyd. You buy Red Oaks and I'll come to visit." She gave him an impish look. "And Peaches and I will beat you then, too."

He reached out and swiped the blade of grass from her hand.

"Hey," she protested.

"You need to learn some respect for your elders."

"My elders?" She snorted. "You think a fancy new hat makes you all grown-up?" That all-too-delectable mouth of hers curved.

Roberto eyed her. "You got a problem with my hat?"

"I don't know, but maybe you do." And quick as a flash, she swiped the black Stetson and dashed away, squealing.

He sprinted after her. "Oh, you're gonna be sorry."

"Big talk," she scoffed, clapping the hat on top of her

head. She was willow thin and fleet, feinting one direction and dashing the other, making him give chase until both of them were laughing and out of breath, circling the red oak that crowned the top of the hill.

"Give it up," he told her as they faced off on either side of a stand of piñon.

She glanced over to Peaches as though judging her distance. "Not a chance." She faked one way and he mirrored her, faked the other. And then she went just a fraction too far and he whipped around the tree and caught her, snaking an arm around her waist to draw her in.

"That's it, *chica,* you're in for it now," he growled.

"Oh, yeah? What are you going to do to me?" There was humor in those soft blue eyes, and mischief and glee. And under it all, something else, something that started the blood rushing in his veins. He caught a hint of scent that made him think of spring and sunshine. He could feel every breath she took. His pulse thundered in his ears.

She wasn't even out of school yet, he reminded himself. He worked for her uncle. He had no business kissing her. Even as his lips hovered over hers, he made himself release her.

And then Frannie leaned in to press her sweet, warm mouth to his.

⊚™ SPECIAL MOMENTS™ 2-in-1

Coming next month

FORTUNE'S WOMAN by RaeAnne Thayne

Ross had his hands full trying to clear his sister's name and look after his nephew. Then Julie Osterman stepped up to help and Ross couldn't resist the lovely counsellor's appeal.

A FORTUNE WEDDING by Kristin Hardy

Years had passed since the one-night fling between Frannie and Roberto. Now Roberto was back, their past secrets exploded into the present – along with a love that couldn't be denied.

⊚

REINING IN THE RANCHER by Karen Templeton

Johnny Griego is blindsided to discover his ex-girlfriend is pregnant. Always responsible, Johnny proposes to Thea. But Thea wants happily-ever-after, not a marriage of convenience…

HIS BROTHER'S SECRET by Debra Salonen

He thought he could arrive in town, make amends for the secrets he kept, then leave. But when Shane Reynard sees Jenna Murphy again, his past longing for her is resurrected…

⊚

HEALING THE MD'S HEART by Nicole Foster

To help his sick son, Duran Forrester would do anything. Then he crossed paths with paediatrician Lia Kerrigan, who has a little TLC for father and son alike!

WELCOME HOME, DADDY by Carrie Weaver

Annie knows her baby deserves a father he can count on. So she's ready to believe that the missing-in-action soldier who fathered her son is dead. Until he shows up on her doorstep…

On sale 19ᵗʰ March 2010

Available at WHSmith, Tesco, ASDA, Eason and all good bookshops.
For full Mills & Boon range including eBooks visit
www.millsandboon.co.uk

SPECIAL MOMENTS™

Single titles coming next month

THE BRAVO BACHELOR

by Christine Rimmer

For Gabe Bravo, sweet-talking young widow Mary into
selling her ranch should have been a cinch. But the
stubborn mum turned the tables and got him to bargain
away his bachelorhood instead!

THE NANNY SOLUTION

by Teresa Hill

Audrey had only been hired to look after Simon's tiny
daughter's dog! But Simon was the perfect boss – and now
his patience and understanding might just prove
impossible for Audrey to resist.

AN IDEAL FATHER

by Elaine Grant

Cimarron is reluctant to become guardian of his orphaned
nephew. But headstrong, gorgeous Sarah James knows
he'd make a great dad. Can this flawed man become
an ideal father?

NOT WITHOUT HER FAMILY

by Beth Andrews

Kelsey is trying to prove her brother's innocence – and
creating nothing but trouble for Jack Martin, chief
of police. Jack should steer clear, but he's
finding Kelsey fascinating…

On sale 19th March 2010

millsandboon.co.uk Community

Join Us!

The Community is the perfect place to meet and chat to kindred spirits who love books and reading as much as you do, but it's also the place to:

- **Get the inside scoop from authors about their latest books**
- **Learn how to write a romance book with advice from our editors**
- **Help us to continue publishing the best in women's fiction**
- **Share your thoughts on the books we publish**
- **Befriend other users**

Forums: Interact with each other as well as authors, editors and a whole host of other users worldwide.

Blogs: Every registered community member has their own blog to tell the world what they're up to and what's on their mind.

Book Challenge: We're aiming to read 5,000 books and have joined forces with The Reading Agency in our inaugural Book Challenge.

Profile Page: Showcase yourself and keep a record of your recent community activity.

Social Networking: We've added buttons at the end of every post to share via digg, Facebook, Google, Yahoo, technorati and de.licio.us.

www.millsandboon.co.uk

2 FREE BOOKS
AND A SURPRISE GIFT

We would like to take this opportunity to thank you for reading this Mills & Boon® book by offering you the chance to take TWO more specially selected books from the Special Moments™ series absolutely FREE! We're also making this offer to introduce you to the benefits of the Mills & Boon® Book Club™—

- **FREE home delivery**
- **FREE gifts and competitions**
- **FREE monthly Newsletter**
- **Exclusive Mills & Boon Book Club offers**
- **Books available before they're in the shops**

Accepting these FREE books and gift places you under no obligation to buy, you may cancel at any time, even after receiving your free books. Simply complete your details below and return the entire page to the address below. You don't even need a stamp!

YES Please send me 2 free Special Moments books and a surprise gift. I understand that unless you hear from me, I will receive 5 superb new stories every month, including a 2-in-1 book priced at £4.99 and three single books priced at £3.19 each, postage and packing free. I am under no obligation to purchase any books and may cancel my subscription at any time. The free books and gift will be mine to keep in any case.

Ms/Mrs/Miss/Mr _____ Initials _____

Surname _____

Address _____

_____

_____ Postcode _____

Send this whole page to: Mills & Boon Book Club, Free Book Offer, FREEPOST NAT 10298, Richmond, TW9 1BR